Just Be Gorgeous

ALSO BY BARBARA WERSBA

For Young Adults

Beautiful Losers
Love Is the Crooked Thing
Fat: A Love Story
Crazy Vanilla
The Carnival in My Mind
Tunes for a Small Harmonica

For Younger Readers

Twenty-Six Starlings Will Fly Through Your Mind
The Crystal Child

A novel by
BARBARA WERSBA

Just Be
Gorgeous

HARPER & ROW, PUBLISHERS
Cambridge, Philadelphia, San Francisco, St. Louis, London, Singapore, Sydney
NEW YORK

Just Be Gorgeous

Typography by Joyce Hopkins
1   2   3   4   5   6   7   8   9   10
First Edition

Library of Congress Cataloging-in-Publication Data
Wersba, Barbara.
    Just be gorgeous.

    "A Charlotte Zolotow book."
    Summary: Feeling unattractive, untalented, and
misunderstood by her parents, a New York City teenager
realizes that she is someone special through her
friendship with a homeless street performer.
    [1. Self-respect—Fiction.   2. Friendship—Fiction.
3. Parent and child—Fiction.   4. New York (N.Y.)—
Fiction]   I. Title.
PZ7.W473Ju   1988   [Fic]   87-45858
ISBN 0-06-026359-8
ISBN 0-06-026360-1 (lib. bdg.)

Just Be Gorgeous

1

It was the first significant thing my mother ever said to me—and I was six years old at the time and acting in the school's Thanksgiving play. The play was all about Pilgrims landing at Plymouth Rock, and guess who I was? Right. The rock. Miss Cummings, the kindergarten teacher, had made me a very convincing costume out of gray burlap—and the thing I remember most about it is that it itched.

So there I was onstage, ready an hour ahead of time for my theatrical debut, when my mother appeared, wearing her mink coat and jangling her four gold bracelets from Tiffany's. You could hear her coming a mile away, like a moving hardware store. She made her entrance onto the stage, where I was standing alone, looked at my costume and hugged me. "It doesn't matter what part you're playing," she whispered in my ear. "Just be gorgeous."

Who but Shirley Rosenbloom could ignore the fact that I wasn't playing a Pilgrim maiden, but a rock. And who but Shirley could say to me afterwards, "You were *wonderful*, baby. You looked great." In other words, who but my mother could look at a rock and see a future Marilyn Monroe? From the minute I was born all she could see was a star, a beauty, a femme fatale—when in reality I have always been a klutz. Short, plump, and insecure. A person whose nose is too big and whose eyes are too small. A person with a voice like Woody Allen's.

The funny thing is that I accepted my mother's obsession as being perfectly normal. Then one day, when I was thirteen, it dawned on me that her attitude was a little bent. I mean, look at it this way: Do you think it is normal for a mother to spend hours doing her daughter's hair? Putting makeup on her daughter? Do you think it is normal for a mother to drag her short, klutzy daughter from department store to department store, trying to find just the right clothes, the right shoes, the right jewelry? Do you think it is normal for a mother to give her only child, for Christmas, a gift certificate to a beauty salon?

"Look what happened to Yvonne De Carlo," my mother would say, as she blow-dried my hair into yet another new style. Meaning, of course, that Yvonne ▪ De Carlo—whose movies I had never seen—had let herself go, had gotten fat and old, and was now doing a TV commercial for a product that kept one's false teeth from falling out. "Remember Yvonne De Carlo," my mother would say, as she tried Peach Blush on my cheeks, as she dabbed my eyelids with Blue Velvet eye shadow. "It could happen to any of us."

My name, by the way, is Heidi Rosenbloom, and my mother and I live in the East 80's in New York City. My parents are divorced, but you would never know it because they spend hours on the phone every week—arguing, discussing, debating every topic from the weather to my latest dentist bill. "What do you mean, five hundred dollars?" my father would scream into the phone. "How can one tooth cost five hundred dollars?"

"The tooth needed a crown," my mother would explain patiently.

"For five hundred I could have bought her a real crown," my father replied. "Besides, who looks that closely at teeth? What is she, a race horse?"

My father's name is Leonard, and he has a jewelry business on West 47th Street. Since he and my mother got divorced, he has lived in Greenwich Village where he pretends to be a swinger, but where—in reality—he just lives a lonely bachelor life. My mother has him over to our apartment on holidays, and I see him every weekend. More about this later.

Shirley Rosenbloom had reached the age of forty-six without realizing that Women's Lib had not only arrived, but that it was here to stay. To her, the whole point of being born female was to trap a man into marriage. And to do that, one had to be beautiful. The fact that she, Shirley, had spent her whole life becoming beautiful only to *lose* her man had never occurred to her. A woman was put on earth to get married and have someone else pay the bills. In return for which, she would provide sex and good housekeeping.

My dad had split when I was twelve and now—at sixteen—living with my mother was becoming intolerable for me. All she ever talked about was my hair and my figure and my wardrobe. And all she ever asked me was why I didn't date more often. Once, trying to tell her the naked truth, I had said, "The reason I don't date *more*, Mother, is that I don't date at all. Boys don't like me. And anyway, most people go out in groups."

Shirley gazed at me as though I had just grown an extra head. "Are you trying to upset me, Heidi?"

"No. Of course not."

"Trying to give me a migraine?"

"No, Mom, no!"

"Then don't say such foolish things to your mother. Boys are crazy about you. They always have been."

"I haven't had a date for a year."

She looked at me suspiciously. "What about that

6

boy who lives downstairs, on the third floor. David. You went to the movies with him."

"David is twelve. He's a child."

Shirley resolved this easily. "Men like older women," she explained. "They like experience."

On and on. To the point where I knew that as long as I lived, I would never communicate with her. Because Shirley Rosenbloom was living in a world gone by, a world of dates and proms and moonlit nights and Yvonne De Carlo movies. A world where virginity was a bargaining chip, and where men married women because they wanted to sleep with them and could not find any other way to do it.

Shirley had grown up in Larchmont, New York, in the 1950's—in an atmosphere where a girl's greatest ambitions were to marry a dentist and have live-in help. Boys had taken her to country club dances and given her corsages. She had kissed the opposite sex good-night at the door and gone inside to her mother—to share every detail of the evening and receive advice on future evenings. She had been a virgin when she married and had gone to Bermuda on her honeymoon. And here's where it gets complicated. Because my grandmother went on the honeymoon too.

Yep, my mother's mother, Rosalie Kantor, went along for the ride. And the crazy thing is that nobody thought this was odd—except my father, of course. And to the end of Rosalie's life my mother called her every day, and took her to lunch every week, and was heartbroken when she died. All of which was amazing, since my grandmother was a tyrant. Time passed. My father bought my mother a Mercedes. They rented a house in the Hamptons every summer, and they had a series of maids, all of whom quit because my mother was so fanatically neat. One speck of dust on a tabletop was enough to give her a nervous breakdown. One dirty ashtray in the living room was enough to bring tears. Then, when my mother was thirty and had given up all hope of having a child, I was born—a fat, ugly baby who everyone thought was adorable. A *mean* baby, who cried a lot, and went to a progressive nursery school, and who was given everything she wanted. Except understanding, of course. But should you ask for the moon?

Shirley was a good wife and a good mother, a terrific cook, a chic dresser, a great hostess—and yet my father left her. He left her for a horse's ass named Jane Anne Mosley, age twenty-four, but that too comes later.

Shirley had many illusions these days, but the worst one was that the education I was receiving—at The Spencer School, on 86th Street—was superior. "Look, what can I tell you," she would say to her friends over the phone. "The school is costing Leonard ten thousand a year. For that, she should be getting *something*, right?"

Wrong. Because Spencer, where I had gone since seventh grade, was nothing more than a country club, a place where you could get away with anything, and a place where the teachers were all young, and impoverished, and underqualified. Also, what my mother did not realize was that the world of private schools was no longer something out of a Nancy Drew book. She thought it was all tea dances and chaperones, whereas in reality it was all sex and coke, and going to bars with phony I.D.'s. One girl in my class, Mitzi Boundwell, had slept with so many boys that she was thinking of becoming a professional. "Why should I be giving it away when I could have a bank account?" she said to me. "When I could be playing the stock market?"

"You must keep yourself pure for the man you will marry," my mother would say dreamily. "You must keep yourself pure, and special, and lovely. Oh baby, I can see such a future for you! And it's filled with roses."

But as far as I was concerned, the roses had died long ago.

So there I was, sixteen years old and a wreck. Not just physically, but spiritually too. I had about as much self-confidence as a dying albatross, and my life was going nowhere. Everyone else I knew was thinking about college, or having a love affair, or deciding to become a computer scientist. Whereas I, Heidi, was turning into some terrible kind of loner—a person who sat in the movies on weekends, and who took long walks by the East River. My best friend, Veronica Bangs, had moved to California last year. I was not dating anyone. I could not imagine the future. The *only* thing I had ever been interested in was dogs, but there didn't seem to be much substance in that. I mean, between the ages of ten and thirteen I had tried to rescue every stray dog in New York. And when that failed, I had offered my services to the ASPCA. They had turned me down because of my age, but The Stray, as a genre, was a big thing to me.

While my mother wanted me to become the next Miss America, my father had always insisted that I become an intellectual. Someone who goes to an Ivy League college and majors in physics. Someone who would acquire several Ph.D.'s by the time she was thirty. *She* wanted me to be Marilyn Monroe, and *he* wanted me to be Albert Einstein—and between the two of them, they were destroying me.

"The unexamined life is not worth living," my Ancient History teacher had said in a seminar last month. So I was examining mine these days, and what I was coming up with was zero. My intellect was no good, and my looks were no good, and I was a virgin. Suicide? No, I said to myself, you're not brave enough. If only you were Catholic, you could become a nun.

10

"Are there any Jewish nuns?" I asked our Religion teacher, Mr. Wannings, one day. But he was so astonished by this question that he could only stare at me.

"Maybe I could be a vet," I said to my friend Veronica, on the long-distance phone one evening. "You know how I love dogs."

"Wow," said Veronica. "Can you see your mother swallowing that one?"

"What about a massage therapist? Shirley has a massage once a week, and the woman who comes to the house is fantastic. I mean, she's very much into the holistic movement and everything. She does shiatsu."

"What's that?"

"I don't know, exactly. But she's an interesting person."

"I haven't spoken to you for a month—and here we are, talking about masooses."

"*Masseuses,*" I corrected her. "Never mind. It's just that I feel so directionless."

"Look," said Veronica, "you're only sixteen. Why should you have your whole life figured out?"

"Because of Shirley. Because of Leonard."

"Well, to hell with them. Why should they bully you that way? *My* mother leaves me alone."

Right, I wanted to say, because she goes out with a million men and is so busy with her lovers that she hardly notices you. But of course I didn't say that.

"When does your Christmas vacation start?" I asked.

"Next week," said Veronica. "God, this is a weird place. All the Christmas trees on Hollywood Boulevard are pink."

"Pink? How come?"

"Because that's how it is out here," she said irritably. "Pink Christmas trees, girl Santas, and fake reindeer outside Grauman's Chinese Theater. They're made of polystyrene."

"I can't afford this phone call," I said to her. "I think we should hang up."

After we hung up, I walked over to the full-length mirror in my room and took a look at myself. And what I saw was neither Marilyn Monroe nor Albert Einstein. What I saw was a very short female who was so nondescript that she could have melted into any crowd in the world. Yes, in any city on this globe, I, Heidi Rosenbloom, could merge in with the masses and never be noticed. There was not one interesting or unusual thing about me. I was a zero.

12

2

"There's a sale on at Lord and Taylor," my mother said, peering into the newspaper. "Fake furs."

"No kidding?" I said, trying to concentrate on my copy of *Massage News*, given to me by Shirley's massage therapist, Gladys.

"We should go down there today, baby. A fake fur would look adorable on you."

"Mother, please. I'm trying to read."

It was Saturday morning, the start of my Christmas vacation, and we were sitting at the dining table finishing our coffee. Knowing that I would be free for three weeks made Shirley restless. She wanted to work on me.

"Listen to this!" she announced. "This week, at the Holiday Inn in Rye, there's going to be a get-together for six hundred singles. What an idea!"

"So why don't you go?" I said with a touch of irony. "It sounds great."

Shirley's face fell. "I was thinking of *you*, sweetie. That it might be fun for you."

"God!" I exploded. "I'm not a 'single,' Mother. Singles are older people."

"OK, OK, forget it. But why don't we go shopping today? You need a few things."

"I'm seeing Daddy this afternoon. For lunch."

Shirley sighed, a drawn-out sigh that was just a little too theatrical. "OK, forget it."

She was still in her robe, a long, peach satin affair with lace on the sleeves—a robe that I had hated for the last five years. It made her look like Joan Bennett. In one of those old movies.

"When you see your father," Shirley said to me, "you can tell him that the alimony check is late again. And that if this continues, I'm phoning Sidney."

Sidney is my mother's lawyer, and calling him is one of her big threats.

"Mom, please don't pull me into this. I don't want to talk money with him."

"You can tell him that I'm not putting up with this nonsense. Not with him living in the lap of luxury. Not with him taking trips all over the globe."

All of which was a little bent, since my father had not traveled in years and was living in a tiny apartment in the Village.

14

My mother gazed at me as though I was something she was thinking of buying at Lord and Taylor. "You know, I think we should streak your hair—just the slightest, tiniest streak of blond. It would be adorable."

I rose to my feet, dropping my copy of *Massage News*. "I'm getting out of here. I've had it."

My mother looked distraught. "So what did I say *this* time? Really Heidi, you are becoming very difficult."

"I'm going out for a walk. And then I'm meeting Daddy for lunch."

I marched into the foyer, where I rummaged around in the closet for a garment that my mother called That Coat. That Coat, as a matter of fact, had become a bone of contention between us— because the coat was a man's coat that I had bought at a thrift shop, a brown-and-black checked overcoat, that on a man might come down to the knees and be considered sporty. On me, of course, it came down to the ankles. The coat was frayed, but it had a terrific brown satin lining, and all kinds of little pockets on the inside. I loved it and had been wearing it since October. But it drove Shirley wild.

"I will not have you going to lunch with your father in that coat," she said, following me into the foyer. "It looks demented."

I said nothing. I simply kept on buttoning my coat.

"What will your father think, with you in such a coat?"

And still, I said nothing.

"He will think that I'm neglecting you," said Shirley. "He will think that we're bums."

"Mother," I said in a cold voice, "I'm wearing the coat. This is my coat, and I'm wearing it."

"Well then, at least put on a little makeup. Don't make him think that we're living like animals."

"Good-bye. I'm going. Good-bye and good luck."

Tears came into Shirley's eyes—those fake tears that she uses every time she wants to get her own way. "Why do you make me look like a bad mother? I devote my *life* to you, and then you go down to your father looking like a derelict."

"So long," I said. "Au revoir."

My words were jaunty, but as I rode down in the elevator my heart was not. Because I had been trying out this defiant attitude for a few months now, and all it produced was trouble. I had hit bottom in October, when Shirley had taken me to Elizabeth Arden's beauty salon for a "re-creation"—a process that consisted of a facial scrub, a permanent, and a makeup analysis. Ever since that experience, I had been rebellious about everything.

However. With Shirley, small rebellions could cause enormous consequences. Like her having a fake heart attack and being rushed to Lenox Hill Hospital. Like killer migraines. And like—just once—

a threat of suicide. I had announced that I was about to cut my hair short, and Shirley had grown so distraught that she opened her bedroom window and leaned out. We live on the fifteenth floor. "You cut off your beautiful hair," she screamed, "and I will throw myself out of this window! And then, Heidi, *then* you will have to explain to your father how it all happened."

Jake, the elevator man, was eyeing my overcoat as we slid down the fifteen floors to the lobby. "I see you're wearing that coat again," he said.

"Right you are if you think you are," I replied. It was the title of a play.

It was starting to snow as I hit the street, a soft powdery December snow, so I reached in my pocket, took out my wool seaman's cap, and pulled it down over my ears. I walked over to Park Avenue and all the little Christmas trees were lit, an aisle of sparkling trees going all the way down to the Pan Am Building—and for some reason, those trees depressed the hell out of me. I thought back to my experience at Elizabeth Arden's, in which I had been poked and prodded, shampooed, toweled, permed, sprayed, scrubbed and creamed. I thought of the beautician saying to my mother, "She's difficult, isn't she?" I remembered how I had looked three hours later when Shirley and I emerged from the salon. Like a female impersonator.

I walked down Park Avenue as the snow got

thicker and thicker, and I felt depression washing over me in waves. So I stepped out into the traffic and hailed a cab—cabs being one of my weaknesses. "Merry Christmas," I said to the driver.

He turned and looked at me as I got into the vehicle. "That's some coat," he said. "Where do you want to go?"

3

My father was waiting for me when I arrived at Giorgio's Restaurant in the West Village, and I knew at once that he had had a drink because his face was flushed. I took my cap off, kissed him, and sat down at the table. Yes, there was an empty martini glass in front of him. And he was smoking again.

My father, who is forty-eight, is very handsome—a person with steel-gray hair and green eyes. He's not tall, but he is a snappy dresser, and though Shirley calls him a womanizer, he isn't. Jane Anne Mosley was his only extramarital affair. He patted my cheek, and I'll say this much for him, he didn't mention the coat.

"How's my baby?" he said. "How's my girl?"

"Fine," I said.

19

"I've ordered fettucini Alfredo for the two of us. Is that all right?"

"Sounds great. How was your week?"

He sighed. "Business is terrible. And at Christmastime, too. I can't understand it."

I took this statement with a grain of salt, because Leonard is one of those men who is always telling you that business is terrible when it's really booming. When I was little I used to love going to his office, which is in an old building on 47th Street, because going to Leonard's office is like going to the White House or something. An armed guard outside the door, and a glass booth where you have to give your name to a receptionist. The security, of course, is because my father buys and sells jewels. He doesn't have an actual store—he just buys and sells from his suite of offices—and when I was little the thing that used to fascinate me was that Leonard would walk around the place with diamonds and rubies in his pockets. They made a clicking sound when he walked.

"I didn't get your report card in the mail," he said to me. "Doesn't it come in December?"

"Yes. It'll come soon."

He ordered another martini and smiled. "So how were your grades, pussycat? Tell the old man the truth."

Inwardly I groaned, because my fall grades had

been rotten. "I did pretty well in English. And also, Ancient History."

Leonard sighed again. "I know, pussycat, I know. But it's your math I'm concerned about. Your science. How are you going to make a good college if you don't have the math, the sciences?"

"I don't know," I said sadly. "Could I have a Coke please?"

Leonard ordered me a Coke and then he shook his head. "I got that doctor bill from your mother, and I almost fainted. Where does she go for checkups, the Mayo Clinic?"

I have forgotten to mention that Leonard pays all of our medical bills, in addition to my mother's alimony. It drives him wild.

"Dr. MacLaren is awfully good," I said tentatively. "And he *is* our family doctor."

"Baby, the days of your mother going to Park Avenue doctors has got to end. The doctor *I* go to is on West Twenty-third Street."

"Well . . ."

"You know that I paid for her psychiatrist when the marriage broke up. And you know that I paid to have her teeth capped. But I just can't afford it any longer."

I cannot stand my father talking about money this way, and so to change the subject, I said, "What have you been doing with yourself, Dad?"

He shrugged. "I don't know. I work late at the office, and then I go to a Chinese restaurant over on Forty-ninth Street. Some nights, I go to a foreign film. That's about it, sweetheart."

It was Jane Anne Mosley who started my father going to foreign films, and as I remembered that, my mind skimmed back over the two years of my father's affair with her. The whole thing was so bizarre that to this day I have trouble sorting it out. Psychologically, I mean. Because Jane Anne Mosley was twenty-four when my father met her—an avant-garde writer who had sold one short story to *The New Yorker* and who thought she was the cat's meow. Tall and blond. Long hair. Piercing eyes. They met because she had a piece of jewelry to sell and someone had given her Leonard's name. Poor Daddy. He fell head over heels for her, and started an affair—all of which we could have endured except that he was so in awe of her. And why? Because of that one asinine story she had published in *The New Yorker*. It was very cryptic, just three pages, and it made no sense to me because it was all about a man who didn't like grapefruit.

Jane Anne lived in the East Village, and after six months Leonard moved in with her. It was so unlike him, because he is really a conservative person, but he admired Jane Anne to the point of insanity. As for Jane Anne—you may well ask—what did she want with Leonard? God, who knows. Maybe he was a father figure or something. Or maybe it was just that he paid her bills.

My parents got a legal separation, and after a year Leonard took Jane Anne and me out to lunch together. It was a disaster, because she treated me like a very tiny child—which I was not, I was thirteen—and I treated her with total coldness. I mean, I did not say one word during the entire luncheon. "How could you have been so rude to her?" my father asked me the next day on the phone. "She was devastated."

Fat chance. Because Jane Anne was the kind of person who would not have been devastated by an atomic bomb. She was a *cool* lady, and calculating, and, as far as I could tell, out for what she could get. But you see, Leonard has always been starved intellectually, and here was this young writer who took him to off-Broadway plays and outdoor concerts. All of a sudden, Leonard was subscribing to *The New York Review of Books*. All of a sudden he was interested in string quartets. And why did Shirley let me go to lunch with them? Because she was so curious. She just had to know what Leonard's girlfriend was like, she just had to know the nature of the competition.

I came home that day, after the doomed luncheon, to find Shirley lying in bed with a cloth over her eyes. "So tell me," she said in a choked voice. "Tell me everything."

To make a long story short, my mother divorced Leonard because of Jane Anne Mosley—getting a hefty alimony allotment, plus my education and our medical bills—only to have the plot take another twist. Because no sooner was the divorce in progress than Jane Anne sold her second story to *The New Yorker*, fell in love with her editor there, and moved in with *him.* Leaving Leonard in pieces. Leaving my mother, who had never wanted a divorce, in pieces too. But somehow it was too late for them to get back together—too many bitter things had been said—and so the divorce went through and Leonard went to live in his sad little Village apartment.

"... tutoring in math," my father was saying. "I would be willing to pay for that."

"Huh?" I said, swinging back to the present. "Excuse me?"

"I said, sweetheart, that I would be willing to pay for some tutoring. Your grades have got to be better than they were last year."

Our meal arrived and we ate it in silence, each lost in his own thoughts. What Leonard was thinking about, I do not know—but my own mind was flashing back to him and Jane Anne living in her tiny apartment on East 7th Street. Yes, I went there once—and it was all books and no furniture, and Mozart on the stereo, and dried flowers in jars. And it was then that I vowed never to become an intellectual. No siree, not if Jane Anne was representative of the tribe. No way.

Leonard ordered coffee and cheesecake for the two of us. He lit a cigarette and sighed again. It was his tenth sigh since I had arrived. "Would you like to come over to the apartment?" he asked. "We could listen to music."

I thought of my father's messy apartment on 13th Street and shuddered. I thought of the piles of laundry on the floor, and the magazines scattered everywhere, and the coffee cups and dirty ashtrays. For a moment, I felt like my mother. "Uh, no thanks. I have some reading to do for next term. A Russian novel."

He nodded approvingly. "Good, good. I want you to be a reader. Your mother, you know, never opened a book in her life.'

So what? I wanted to scream. Because the way each of them talks about the other drives me insane. "His habits are *foul*," Shirley would say to me. "Not a brain in her head," Leonard would declare. I'm making light of all this, but it hurts me, you know. It really does.

We stood on the sidewalk in the blowing snow, and Leonard put his arms around me. "I miss you. I wish we could be together more."

"Sure," I said. "I know."

"Do your homework for next term, pussycat. Don't waste these next weeks."

"Right," I replied.

"And tell your mother, no more Park Avenue doctors. I mean that."

"Absolutely."

"I love you, baby," said Leonard, hugging me. But I was like a block of cement.

As usual, he had slipped a ten-dollar bill in my hand as we parted, and so I hailed another cab. And as the cab crawled uptown through the snow, I imagined all the questions that Shirley would ask me about the luncheon. What was Leonard wearing and how many martinis had he drunk? Did he look thin? Were there circles under his eyes? Did he mention dating anyone? Had he stopped smoking?

What she really wanted to know, of course, was: Is he miserable? But that, I was not about to tell her.

"They use me like a Ping-Pong ball," I said aloud.

"Beg pardon?" said the driver.

"My parents," I said to him, "are divorced, and they use me like a goddam Ping-Pong ball. It's killing me."

"Don't take it so hard," said the driver. "There are worse things."

Yeah? I wanted to reply. Like what?

And it was then, for some reason, that I decided to cut my hair. Very very short.

4

It was two days later and I was being massaged in our living room by Gladys, the massage therapist. She was not a *masseuse*, she had said to me last week, she was a *massage therapist*. There was a difference.

The reason I was lying on the massage table, stark naked, with only a towel covering me, was that Shirley was late for her appointment with Gladys. Having gone out shopping, she had not yet returned—and so Gladys had offered to do me instead, for a few minutes, for free.

"Relax, for God's sake," said Gladys. "You're like a rock."

"I'm sorry," I said. I was lying on my back and she was working on my arms. I glanced up at her and saw that Gladys looked wonderful today. She has black hair, which she wears in one long braid, and her skin is very white. She was wearing an interesting loose-knit, yellow sweater.

"God," Gladys said to me, "you're like the Petrified Forest. Don't you ever get any exercise?"

"Not much," I replied. "Except for gym, at school. But you can always get out of that if you want to. People forge their own notes."

"Relax," said Gladys, beginning to work on my neck. "Give in a little. Give yourself to me."

As much as I like Gladys, I could not imagine giving myself to her in any way. "I'll try," I said.

She was working on the sides of my neck, going deeper and deeper into the muscles. It hurt like hell. "How's Vanya?" I asked. Vanya is Gladys's boyfriend—a chef.

"He's beautiful. Relax, Heidi. Try to enjoy what I'm doing."

It was like asking someone to enjoy the guillotine, but I tried.

"Yes!" Gladys said. "That's it! That's better. We're breaking through."

"Gladys," I said, as she stood behind me, reached under my shoulder blades, and began to dig away, "what would you do if you were a person without looks, personality, talent or intellect?"

"I'd shoot myself," Gladys replied.

"Maybe I could be a car shepherd," I said pensively.

"What? Relax, Heidi, please."

"A car shepherd is a person who moves your car from one side of the street to the other. You know. On one side of the street the sign says parking from twelve to six, or something, and on the other side of the street the sign says parking from six to ten. Or whatever. So a car shepherd gets paid for moving people's cars around."

"I don't have a car. I know nothing about it."

"A boy in my class, Peter Applebaum, is a car shepherd. His father took away his allowance when he caught him dealing drugs, so Peter is a car shepherd now. He makes two hundred dollars a month."

"And for that you kids go to private school? Amazing. Turn over now, Heidi, on your stomach."

I turned over, trying to retain my modesty via the bath towel, and Gladys began to work on my lower back.

"The thing about being a car shepherd," I continued, "is that it doesn't require any special education. And since there are more and more cars in the city, and more and more parking problems, you'd never be out of work."

"Myself, I taught jazz dancing for ten years," said Gladys.

"Then why did you become a therapist?"

"A long story, kid. A very long story."

In the silence that followed, I thought about Peter Applebaum, on whom I once had a big crush. Peter was neither a jock nor a brain, a loner or a socializer, an extrovert or introvert. No siree, Peter Applebaum was a crook. He stole from department stores, dealt dope, and was once even arrested for breaking into his dentist's office to let a friend use the laughing gas—for a fee, of course. And how could I have had such a big crush on such a lousy person? Easy. He was—in the words of my mother—gorgeous.

"Gladys," I said, "how many years does it take to become a massage therapist?"

"Two years at the Institute—and believe me, it's tough. You have to learn as much anatomy as a doctor. More, maybe."

Which lets *me* out, I thought. Anatomy is not my best subject. So it was either becoming a car shepherd or a bicycle messenger. New York is full of the latter and they make pretty good money.

Suddenly, Shirley burst into the room, swathed in mink, her arms filled with packages. "Sorry!" she said. "I couldn't get a cab. Well, for goodness' sake, baby, are you having a massage?"

"Yes," I said in a muffled voice. My face was buried in the leather table.

"It's like working on Mount Rushmore," Gladys said to my mother. "Why is she so tense?"

Shirley dropped her packages and took off her mink. "She's not tense!" she said gaily. And then, to me: "Baby, you won't believe what I bought you at Saks."

I got off the massage table and put on my robe. My mother was ripping open a large box.

"Voilà!" said Shirley, pulling something satiny out of the box. It was a pink satin nightgown.

"Very pretty," said Gladys, tactfully.

"Mother," I said in a weak voice, "you know I don't wear nightgowns. I wear pajamas."

"I know, I know," she said cheerfully, "but I thought it was time for a change. There was a sale on nightgowns, and this one is just your size. Try it on for us, baby. For Gladys and me."

I had not meant to scream at my mother, but it was a scream that came out. "No!" I screamed. "I won't! I am not Jean Harlow, Mother! I am not a French prostitute! I wear pajamas. With elephants on them."

"Well, for God's sake," said Shirley, "you don't have to yell at me. I thought I was doing something nice for you."

"She thought she was doing something nice," said Gladys.

To my amazement, there were tears in my eyes. Before anyone could notice them, I left the room. "Well, for God's sake . . ." I could hear Shirley saying.

I went into my room, slammed the door, and put on a pair of old corduroy pants and a sweater, jogging shoes and That Coat—which was lying on the bed. Then I marched through the living room. My

31

mother was on the massage table, with a towel over her, and Gladys was saying, ". . . a phase, that's all. Kids go through phases."

I went down in the elevator with Jake, the elevator man, and though I do not smoke I asked him for a cigarette. He gave me a Kool, lit it for me, and with the cigarette hanging out of my mouth I stormed out of the building.

We live near Lexington Avenue, and on Lexington and 82nd there is a barber shop. So I made my way there, puffing on the cigarette, and went through the door. "Yes, miss?" said one of the barbers. "Can I help you?"

"Yes," I said, "you can. I want my hair cut off. All of it."

The barber looked at my long black curly hair, and shook his head dubiously. "I don't know, young lady. I think a beauty parlor would be better for you."

"No," I declared, "I don't need a beauty parlor. I just want my hair cut off. Very very short."

The man shrugged and led me over to a barber chair. There were two other customers, male, having their hair cut—and they stared at me as though I had invaded their turf. I did not give a damn, however. I just wanted to rid myself of some part of the old Heidi Rosenbloom.

"Short," I said to the barber. "Very very short."

5

"You wouldn't be so calm if you could see her!" my mother screamed into the phone. "She looks like a convict!"

"So what?" my father was saying. "It's only hair, for God's sake."

"Who will date her, looking like that? Who will marry her?"

There was a sputtering sound on the other end of the phone—yes, I was listening on the extension—making me know that Leonard was at the end of his rope. "*Marry her?* She's only sixteen years old, Shirley. What do you want, a child bride?"

"You are deliberately misunderstanding me! Deliberately trying to make a fool of me. I'm telling you that she went to a barber shop and had her beautiful hair butchered. When she was little, I brushed that hair by the hour, making it gorgeous."

"Hair grows back," said my father. "Unlike fingers and toes, hair grows back. Let her do what she wants."

"In every argument, every crisis, you take her side," Shirley said with a sob. "It's like I don't exist."

"I have to go now," Leonard said in a cold voice. "And I wish you wouldn't call me at the office. It's embarrassing."

"Oh yes, oh yes," Shirley sobbed, "I'm nothing but an embarrassment now. Me, who saw you through the hard times, who stood by you when you were drinking too much. Now, suddenly, I'm an embarrassment."

I winced, because I was sure that Shirley's speech was straight out of a soap opera she watched every day. It was called *My Secret Destiny*.

"I'm hanging up now," said Leonard. "Goodbye."

I put down the receiver of the extension phone and hurried into my room. For the fifth time that morning, I went over to the mirror and looked at myself. Before, I had been a nonentity with long hair. Now I was a nonentity with a crew cut. And yet . . . there was something nice about it. The way it felt when I passed my hand over it. The way I could wash it in the shower and then towel it dry in a few minutes. My head felt like Maxie, the old French

34

Poodle we used to have. He had been our only dog because Shirley insists she is allergic to animals, and Poodles don't shed.

I turned and gave my room a long, hard look. Shirley had redecorated this room for me two years ago, and I guess the model she had had in mind was a ladies' lounge in a department store. Or a beauty salon. Because my room was all pale pink and baby blue. All chintz, and patterned wallpaper, with a fussy dressing table on which she had placed little bottles of perfume. There was a pink velvet boudoir chair and a full-length mirror in a gilt frame. She had placed large photos of Leonard and herself, in the old days, on my desk. The bed was a four-poster one, with a frilly pink bedspread. Yes, the whole thing was like a beauty salon. And the more I stared at it, the sicker I felt.

My childhood possessions were in the closet—Shirley having no tolerance for them anymore—and from time to time I would take them out and look at them. An old Kodak camera, and a xylophone given to me one Christmas by Leonard. My teddy bear, Sweetpea, my roller skates, and dozens of books on dogs. The history of the German Shepherd. An illustrated guide to Dachshunds. Books on dog psychology and dog diseases. A rare book called *Alpine Dogs of World War II*.

Without knocking, Shirley charged into the room.

35

She was wearing her peach satin robe and had her hair up in rollers. "Your father is *sick* about what you have done to yourself," she announced. "I just talked to him and he's shocked."

"No kidding."

Wearily, she sat down on the velvet chair. "First, that man's coat and now the hair. What is the point of it all? To make me look like a fool?"

"Why should my looks make *you* look like a fool?"

"Your hair is a disgrace, Heidi. You know that."

"I like it this way. It feels good—like Maxie used to feel."

"You're comparing yourself to a dog? A poodle who had fleas?"

"Maxie never had fleas," I said, my anger rising. "I used to bathe him myself."

"I hated that dog. I'm glad he's gone."

And that's when I fell apart.

"I'm getting out of here!" I yelled. "I'm going out for the whole day, and maybe the whole night too. Because I can't take this anymore, Mother. I just can't!"

"Take what, take what?" she said in confusion. "Oh God, Heidi, what's the matter *now*? You're hysterical because I said something about *Maxie*?"

But I was halfway across the living room, wearing That Coat, and jeans, and jogging shoes. I grabbed my wool seaman's cap off the coatrack and slammed the door.

I walked over to Fifth Avenue, boarded a bus that was so crowded you could hardly breathe, and stood in the aisle with anger pounding inside of me. Until a few months ago I had simply been Heidi Rosenbloom—a kind of mannequin on whom her mother kept trying out new lives. The life of a model, the life of a movie star, the life of a jet-setter. And I had been so paralyzed that I had given in to all this. But now . . . now a new Heidi Rosenbloom was emerging. The trouble was, I had no idea who she would be. "Without looks or talent, personality or intellect, what should a person do?" I said aloud.

"What?" said a fat lady standing next to me.

"Nothing," I replied. "Excuse me."

A man got off the bus and I grabbed his seat, which was by the window. And as the bus edged its way down Fifth Avenue, I studied the windows in all the department stores. Yes, there was Tiffany's with glittering jewelry placed in little sleighs, and then the splendor of Steuben, where Shirley bought wedding gifts for people, and finally Saks—with Christmas music coming from loudspeakers and mechanized Christmas scenes in the windows. Dickensian figures smiled and bowed in front of little fireplaces. Mechanized dogs wagged their tails. Tiny children opened presents.

All of a sudden it occurred to me that shopping was my mother's religion. Other people might believe in the Pope, but she believed in Bloomingdale's. Other people might go to mass every day. She went to Saks. Because to a woman like Shirley, spending money gave a feeling of peace. In addition to which, a department store was like a second home. I mean, you could not only eat there, but sleep there too—little naps in the ladies' lounge—and you were constantly being rewarded for your presence. Models gave you free bottles of perfume. Your Christmas extravagance was rewarded by Christmas sales. You could even go to a department store and be entertained with a show. Suddenly the store was "doing" the Southwest, with real potters making pottery on the ground floor, and Tex-Mex food being served in the restaurant. Suddenly there were American Indians dancing around the cosmetic counters. Girls in ruffled skirts handed out tamales.

I got off the bus at 48th Street and walked over to Rockefeller Center to look at the Christmas tree. It was very beautiful and very tall, glittering with a thousand little lights, but all I could think of was that some tree had given its life to entertain a lot of people who didn't give a damn about it in the first place. "It's a crime to cut down a tree like that," I said to a cop who was standing nearby.

He shrugged. "Look, what can you do? Life is unfair."

"I know it is. But does the tree know?"

"Huh?"

"Never mind. It's just too bad to kill a tree like that."

I proceeded west, feeling sadder and sadder—but then, Christmas always depressed me. First, because the holidays were the time when most of the Rosenbloom family fights occurred. And second, because we shouldn't have been celebrating Christmas in the first place. We should have been celebrating Chanukah, but for as long as I could remember we had behaved like typical, assimilated New York Jews—having Christmas one day, and going to some kid's bar mitzvah the next.

I walked farther west, toward the Broadway theater district. And as the streets got shabbier and less crowded, I began to feel bad about yelling at Shirley. There was simply no profit in getting mad at her, because she never saw the point of any argument. All she could do was weep, and develop a migraine, and withdraw to her bed. My grandmother, Rosalie, had been the same way.

I decided to buy Shirley two tickets to a musical—as her Christmas present—because, outside of shopping, musicals were her favorite thing. She had not yet seen the revival of *Sweet Charity*, so I decided to try for that one. I stopped at a newsstand, bought a paper, and looked up the theaters. *Sweet Charity* was playing at the Minskoff.

There was a long line for tickets at the Minskoff, a line that stretched out onto the sidewalk, so I took my place in it. The man in front of me, a Wall Street type, looked at my coat and raised his eyebrows. Sorry mister, I said silently. This is my coat and I like it.

It was cold out, really brisk, so I pulled my coat collar up and my wool cap down over my ears. Then I became aware of something. A kid with bleached blond hair was doing a tap dance in the middle of the sidewalk, right in front of the theater. He had placed a tape recorder on the pavement and was dancing to some old Judy Garland tune.

I turned around to watch him, and saw that he had placed a hat on the pavement, for money, and that people were throwing coins into it. God, could he dance! Like a pro. But he was also very weird. That bleached blond hair, and faded jeans, and—yes—a woman's fur jacket that had definitely seen better days. It was one of those ratty fur jackets you can get at any thrift shop. He also had on tap shoes.

The Garland tune he was playing was terrific, and as the boy tapped away, I decided to give him some money. Not just a quarter or a dollar, but something important. I left the line for a minute, and put a five-dollar bill into his hat. Without missing a beat, he smiled at me, said, "Oh my, *thank* you," and kept on dancing. I got back into line, but I kept on watching him. He was very very good.

40

The only available tickets to *Sweet Charity* cost forty-five dollars apiece, and even I, with my good allowance, could not afford that. So I said no thanks to the man in the ticket booth, decided to buy Shirley some records instead, and went back to the street. It was snowing now, but the kid hadn't stopped dancing. And while people were putting coins in his hat, the amounts weren't very generous. I was the only one who had given him a five.

And then I did something strange. Something not like me at all. Something that was about to change my life, though of course I could not have known it at the time. What I did was, I walked up to this person and said, "Can I buy you a cup of coffee?"

Without missing a beat, he said, "Lovely. I'll be with you in a minute."

The music came to an end, the kid stopped dancing, and kneeled down on the sidewalk to gather up his money. It wasn't very much, maybe ten dollars.

"There's a coffee shop down the street," I said to him. "Let's go there."

"Super," he said. "My name's Jeffrey."

"Mine's Heidi," I said. We shook hands.

Jeffrey looked me over, but not in an unpleasant way. It seemed like he was just trying to find out who I was and what I was like—right off the bat. "That's a *divine* coat," he said. "Where did you get it?"

6

We walked down the street to a coffee shop called Danny's, and, in a very gentlemanly way, Jeffrey helped me off with my coat. Then he removed his fur jacket and I saw that all he had on underneath the jacket was a thin white sweatshirt and jeans. What it said on the sweatshirt was this: "Dear Auntie Em, I hate you, I hate Kansas, and I'm taking the dog."

"That's a *wonderful* sweatshirt," I said.

"Isn't it? I bought it in the Village."

"What would you like?" I asked. "My treat."

"Well . . ." Jeffrey replied, and then I realized that he was famished. Don't ask me how I knew this, but I did. "Why don't you have a hamburger?" I suggested. "And then, perhaps, some pie."

His face brightened. "Oh, how nice of you. I will."

The minute the food arrived he wolfed it down, and I had never seen anyone eat that way in my entire life. I don't mean that he had bad manners—it was just that he was starving. "Would you like another burger?" I inquired.

"Can you afford it?"

"Yes. Of course."

"Then I accept," said Jeffrey.

He ate the second burger more slowly, concentrating on it like it was a dish at The Four Seasons. I studied him. Very bleached hair, and—if you can believe this—some pale-blue eye shadow on his lids. I couldn't believe that I had approached him, back at the theater. That I, Heidi, could have had so much chutzpah.

"What's your last name?" I asked, as he finished the second burger.

"Collins," he replied. "Jeffrey Collins. It's only a stage name, but I think it's rather good. Don't you?"

"Yes," I said, "I do. *My* last name is Rosenbloom. I hate it."

"So change it, sweetie. Make it beautiful."

I ordered some pie à la mode for Jeffrey, and a second cup of coffee for myself. "Are you in show business?" I asked.

"Not yet," he said, "but I will be. As soon as I'm discovered. And *that*, my love, is why I'm dancing on the sidewalk. But why not? Piaf sang in the streets for years."

"Who?"

"Piaf. Edith Piaf. The great French chanteuse."

"Oh," I said. "Right."

I was growing more and more interested in him. I mean, there he was, with bleached hair, and wearing a woman's jacket, and yet he had no self-consciousness at all. He seemed honest, and kind of funny. And very nice. "Where are you from?" I asked.

"Chicago. But I left six months ago. I just couldn't stand it anymore."

"Stand what?"

He patted his lips with a paper napkin. "The lifestyle, sweetie. The crassness. The lack of sensitivity. And also, to be brutally frank about it, people kept beating me up."

For some reason, this shocked me. "Really? How come?"

Jeffrey patted his lips again. "Because I'm gay, dear, and gay boys are not too popular on Chicago's South Side. Do you know what some teenagers do there on Saturday nights?"

"Go to bars?" I suggested timidly.

"Right," said Jeffrey. "*First* they go to bars, and then they go fag bashing. In other words, they find some poor soul like me and try to beat him to a pulp."

Well, I was floored. Because while he *was* a little unusual, it had not occurred to me that he was gay.

But on the other hand, this was a subject about which I knew very little. "Did you ever fight back?"

"No," he said, "I didn't. But if it ever happens in New York, I will. I'm sick of being used as a punching bag."

"How old are you?"

"Twenty. Do I look it?"

"No, no," I said quickly, "you look very young. Where are you staying in New York? A hotel?"

"Not exactly, dear. An abandoned building would be more like it."

"Huh?"

"I've tried all the men's shelters, Heidi, and they're dangerous. I mean, my God, you could get murdered there. And people keep trying to steal my tape recorder. So I'm living in an abandoned building on West Fifty-third Street."

I was stunned by this information. Because the weather was freezing. "Do they have heat there?"

"Of course not, sweetie. We wrap up in blankets. There are six of us."

I ordered another cup of coffee and took out a Kool. Quickly, Jeffrey lit it for me. "What's your real name?" I asked.

"Tom Sweeney. Which is why I changed it to something more attractive."

"Are your parents alive?"

"I have no parents, love. I was raised in a couple of foster homes."

"God," I said.

"The problem is that once you're aged out of the system—the welfare system, I mean—they just throw you out on the street. No preparation for life, nothing. You live in foster homes, and get a meager high school education, and then one day you're eighteen and out on your own. I had nowhere to go. I didn't know what to do. So I washed dishes in a restaurant for a while, and then I got a job in a dime store. Would you believe it, until six months ago I was standing behind a counter selling lamps! All I had ever wanted in my life was to be on Broadway, to be a star, yet there I was selling lamps. It was killing me."

"Have you had dancing lessons?"

"No, I could never afford that. I learned to dance and sing from watching old movies on television. Hundreds and hundreds of movies—with Rogers and Astaire, and Gene Kelly, and Judy, and all those wonderful people. I used to pretend that Judy Garland was my mother, that someday she'd come and find me. I mean, she was dead by then, but I pretended all the same."

"Did you ever know your real mother, Jeffrey?"

I could have bitten my tongue, because a look of sadness crossed his face. "No. She gave me up for adoption the day I was born."

"She was very young?"

"Yes. Seventeen."

We were silent for a while, and then I said, "What are your plans? For the future, I mean."

"My plans are to get through this winter without starving, and to attract the attention of a Broadway agent or producer. And where better to attract attention than on the street? Oh, I suppose I could make the rounds, the way the others do, but it's such a waste of time! The agents say, 'It's lovely to see you, dear'—and then the minute you're out the door they throw your photo and resumé into the wastebasket."

"In other words, you're waiting to be discovered."

"Yes, and do you know something funny? I am confident that I will be. I know that I will be discovered for Broadway just as surely as we're sitting here together. I have complete and utter faith."

I stared at him. Because I had never in my life heard anyone say that he had complete and utter faith in anything.

"You're a terrific dancer. I was watching you for a long time."

"It's true," he said softly. "I am."

All of a sudden, I felt like crying. I don't know why. It was just that he only had a little jacket for warmth, and he was living in an abandoned building. And there he was—with complete and utter faith.

"I have no faith in anything," I said. "I'm not like you at all."

Impulsively, Jeffrey grabbed my hand. "Oh, but Heidi, you must! Faith is the foundation of all human life. Without faith a person can't do anything."

"Well, I'm lacking it. I have no faith, or hope, or anything."

"You know," he said, "I spent some time in an orphanage when I was little, and there was this nun there, Sister Margaret, who opened up the world for me. She used to say, 'Tom, there isn't a thing you can't do if you will only set your mind to it.' And she *meant* it. She used to watch me practice my tap dancing in the basement of the orphanage, and she'd applaud and applaud."

"You mean, she encouraged you to go on the stage?"

"I owe everything to her. But that's a story for another time."

"Look," I said after a moment, "why don't you come to dinner on Friday? My mom's a very good cook. And I think you need some regular meals."

Jeffrey winked at me. "You mean, you're bringing me home to mother?"

"Well, yes. Sure."

"Mothers don't always like me, love. Mothers don't always approve."

I thought this over for a moment. "I'll work on her. She's a rather difficult person, but she is a good cook. We usually have beef stew on Fridays."

"Divine. Where do you live?"

I took out a piece of paper and wrote my address down for him. "Come for dinner Friday night. At six."

Jeffrey rose to his feet and stretched. "I have to get back to the theater before the evening performance. You never know who will see you."

"Friday night then," I said. "For dinner."

To my amazement, he leaned over and kissed me on the cheek. "It's a date. And Heidi? I'm just crazy about that haircut of yours. Who cuts it for you?"

7

"Listen to this," said my mother, rattling the newspaper. "Elizabeth Taylor is going into the perfume business. She's going to call her product Passion."

"Isn't there one called Poison too?" I asked.

"Right. Dior makes it."

"Well, maybe the next one they'll come up with will be called Passionate Poison."

My mother glanced at me. "Are you trying to be funny, Heidi?"

"No," I said. "Not at all."

It was the morning after I had met Jeffrey, and Shirley and I were at our usual places at the dining table. Ethel, our latest maid, had just quit—but Shirley had fixed us an interesting brunch of eggs Benedict with asparagus. She was wearing her peach satin robe and gold loop earrings.

"There's a picture of her here, too," said Shirley. "God, she looks good! After being a drug addict all those years, or whatever she was. It just shows you what can happen when a person *tries*."

"Tries what?"

"To be beautiful!" said Shirley, exasperated. "Elizabeth Taylor is beautiful again. She was a mess for years, and now she's beautiful."

All of which made me think about Jeffrey. Not that I had stopped thinking about him since I had wakened at five A.M. The temperature was in the twenties and there was Jeffrey, sleeping in an abandoned building on 53rd Street. The very thought of it hurt my heart.

"Burton, on the other hand, fell apart completely," my mother was saying. "Before he died in Bavaria or someplace, he looked a hundred years old."

She rattled the newspaper and turned to the next page.

It was Wednesday morning. Which meant that I only had two days in which to prepare my mother for Jeffrey. How to do this? The truth about Jeffrey was not going to thrill her, but if I lied too much, that would be dangerous too. I decided to take the middle road. "Mom?" I said tentatively.

"Ummm?"

"Mom, I've met this boy . . ."

Shirley put down the newspaper. She stared at

me, and I saw that her eyes were glittering like a snake's. "What did you say?"

"I've met a boy," I repeated. "His name is Jeffrey and he's from out of town. I invited him to dinner on Friday."

"Well, for God's sake! You never said a word about it."

"I know. I was waiting for the right moment. His name is Jeffrey. He's an actor."

It took a moment for Shirley to weigh this information on the scales of her mind. "An actor? What show is he in? Would I have seen him in something? How did you meet him, Heidi? You've never known any actors before."

Now, I decided, was the moment to lie. "I met him through mutual friends. The trouble is, he's here from out of town, auditioning for a musical, and he doesn't have a place to stay."

"Oh, my God," said Shirley, "I'll have to redecorate the guest room! Why didn't you tell me about this? Does he come from a nice family? Who are his parents?"

"I don't *know* who his parents are. And you don't have to redecorate the guest room. I mean, for heaven's sake, Mother. I only asked him to dinner."

Shirley was on her feet now, pacing the room. "I'll have the carpet man in to shampoo the living-room rug—and maybe Ethel will come back for one night, just to serve dinner. What about filet mignon? And

52

strawberries with Cointreau for dessert."

"Mother . . ."

"And we'll run down to Elizabeth Arden's, to see what they can do with your hair. If worse comes to worse, we can buy you a wig."

"Mother, stop! Please. We don't have to do all that for Jeffrey. He's a very simple person."

"I'll bet," said Shirley. "I'll just bet. No one in the theater is *simple*, baby. I mean, look at Richard Burton, look at Michael Caine. They're highly complicated people. How old is this Jeffrey?"

"Twenty."

"Twenty . . ." she mused. "Four years' difference is not too bad. But Heidi, I have to warn you that theater people are not the most stable types. I wish he was in some other profession."

"God!" I yelled. "I'm not marrying him! I only asked him to dinner!"

"Heidi," said my mother, "calm down. There is no reason to get so excited about this. So a boy is coming to dinner. So what? You think we can't handle such a situation? I'll just have the carpet shampooed and see if Ethel can serve. We'll get your blue dress dry-cleaned."

I am not going to bore you with everything that happened after that. But I did wonder how I could have been so naive. I mean, it was not a normal event for me to have any member of the male sex to dinner, so Shirley went a little insane. She had the carpet man in, and sent my blue dress to the dry cleaners. She had her hair done, cleaned the apartment from top to bottom, and planned a gourmet meal. As for me, I had put my foot down about going to Elizabeth Arden's. Wearing a dress for dinner would be terrible enough.

I am not a person given to prayer, but on Thursday night I sat cross-legged on my bed, closed my eyes, and prayed. And what I prayed for was to have Jeffrey win my mother over. He was the first boy I had liked since Peter Applebaum, and I wanted—so much—for everything to go well. I knew he was gay and all that, but I liked him. There was something about him that got to me.

By five P.M. on Friday, the apartment looked like something out of *House and Garden.* Fresh flowers in the living room, my grandmother's Spanish shawl draped over the piano, and our best silver on the dining table. Shirley was wearing a black dress by Chanel, and three strands of pearls. I was wearing my hated blue dress. Ethel, the maid, had refused to come and serve dinner, but Shirley said she would serve it herself. "We'll all pitch in!" she said. "It will be fun."

By five forty-five Shirley and I were sitting on the couch together. Her mood was very cheerful, but I was so tense I was developing a headache. "Mom . . ." I began.

"Yes, sweetie?" She looked very happy.

I cleared my throat. "Mom . . . I don't want you to expect too much of Jeffrey. I mean, he is not a conventional person. He's a little different from other people."

"So what?" she said gaily. "Theater people are like that. Do you think I don't know?"

Then the doorbell rang.

Shirley and I walked into the foyer. With a flourish, she opened the front door. And there stood Jeffrey—as I had feared—in his blue jeans and little fur jacket. He had his tape recorder and tap shoes with him.

He had brought Shirley a rose.

It was a long-stemmed pink rose, wrapped in cellophane, and Shirley was so excited by it that she saw the rose before she saw Jeffrey. "Mrs. Rosenbloom?" said Jeffrey, proffering the flower. "Good evening. This is for you."

With a little cry of pleasure, Shirley took the long-stemmed rose from Jeffrey. Then she looked at him. She went pale. "You're Jeffrey?"

"None other," he replied.

Jeffrey and I kissed on the cheek. I took his fur jacket, and we all walked into the living room. Shirley's face was the color of ashes. "Heidi," she said in a small voice, "will you come into my bedroom for a minute?"

"There's liquor over on the bar," I said to Jeffrey. "Make yourself a drink."

55

As soon as Shirley and I were alone in her bedroom, she closed the door and locked it. "What is the meaning of this?" she said. "What are you trying to do?"

"Mother . . ."

"I mean, my God! What *is* he? Something out of the circus?"

"Mother, I . . ."

"You tell me you're having a boy over for dinner, and then *this* arrives! What is he, a derelict off the Bowery? A male prostitute?"

Suddenly, like Joan of Arc or someone, I was filled with courage. Because I did not intend to have my mother insult my new friend. And if that meant tying her up and putting a gag over her mouth—and entertaining Jeffrey alone—then I was prepared to do that. But I was not going to let her hurt his feelings.

"Mother," I said, taking her arm, "listen to me. Jeffrey is my new friend, and I will not have you insulting him. He's a nice person, and he's fallen on hard times, and he needs help. All over New York people are sleeping on the streets or in abandoned buildings or something, while *we* live in luxury."

"He's a street person?" Shirley said weakly.

"Yes! From Chicago, and the only person who was ever kind to him was a nun in an orphanage."

Shirley sank down on her bed. "OK," she said, "OK. But you should have told me the truth. You said you had met a boy."

56

"Well, isn't he one?"

"No," said my mother, "he isn't. He's some kind of . . . transvestite or something. He's wearing eye shadow."

"And for that, we're going to turn him away?"

"No," said Shirley, "we won't turn him away. Come on, Heidi, let's go back to the living room."

You could have knocked me over with a feather. Because I didn't think she was going to cooperate. But, to my surprise, Shirley marched back into the living room, where Jeffrey was sipping a glass of sherry, and said, "So, Jeffrey. It's nice to have you here. My daughter tells me you're from Chicago."

8

Ten minutes later the three of us were sitting in the living room. Jeffrey and I were having sherry, while Shirley had her nightly scotch and soda. I'll say this much for Jeffrey, he seemed completely at ease—like he dined in people's apartments every night.

"That's a *stunning* dress," he said to my mother. "May I ask where you bought it?"

Shirley looked surprised. "I got it in Paris long ago. It's a Chanel."

"It's so terribly understated," said Jeffrey. "And so becoming."

There were a few moments of silence, and then Jeffrey exclaimed, "And your apartment, Mrs. Rosenbloom! Such lovely things, such exquisite taste."

"Heidi's father and I used to buy at auction. Most of these pieces are French."

"Your taste is fabulous," said Jeffrey.

Shirley seemed confused. Because on the one hand Jeffrey's looks offended her, but on the other hand his manners didn't. After we had finished our drinks we went into the dining room. Jeffrey stood behind my mother and held her chair.

"Why, thank you Jeffrey," she said.

"My pleasure," he replied.

His manners were beautiful. I mean, he passed the food around as though we were in an English castle, and he kept saying things like, "Thank you, you're very kind," or "How absolutely delicious this is!" Jeffrey, I said to myself, you must have watched a hell of a lot of movies.

Yet there he was, in his faded jeans and white sweatshirt, with his tape recorder and tap shoes in the foyer, and his hair looking more bleached than ever, and his way of saying things in such an exaggerated way that you kept questioning his sincerity—until you realized that he *was* sincere. There he was, with no home and no money and no prospects, right off the street . . . and filled with hope.

Without the slightest self-consciousness, Jeffrey explained to my mother that he was living in an abandoned building on 53rd Street and that he danced in front of theaters all day long. "It's only a matter of time until I'm discovered," he explained.

Shirley looked like she was casting around in her mind for something to ask him—some question that would not seem too personal. "Ah, Heidi tells me that you have a good friend who's a nun."

Jeffrey brightened. "I do! In Evanston. Sister Margaret."

"Amazing," said Shirley.

"I met Sister when I was eight years old, and she knew that I had talent right away. But since there was no chance of my having dancing lessons, she taught me some basic steps—and then she gave me a key to the television room in the orphanage. 'Watch movies,' she said to me. 'Watch them all day long, Tom, and when you see something you like, just imitate it.' "

"Imagine that," said my mother. "A nun being that way."

"She would take me to the neighborhood movie house once a week, and then we'd go back home together and act out all the parts. God, it was fun! She'd be Sophia Loren and I'd be Cary Grant."

"Sophia Loren?" said Shirley. "A nun being Sophia Loren?"

"It was just playacting, but we had such a good time together. I still miss her."

"But you correspond?" I said hopefully.

A sad little smile crossed Jeffrey's face. "I write her, but since I've been moving around a lot lately, there's really no way for her to write *me*."

"Very commendable," said Shirley. "Very nice."

60

We ate the rest of the meal in silence—filet mignon, new potatoes, and Shirley's spinach soufflé—and the minute we were done, Shirley said that she had a headache and needed to lie down. Jeffrey and I put the dishes in the dishwasher, and then I took him into my room. "Here it is," I said. "Here's where I live."

"Oh!" he exclaimed. "Cute, very cute." He paused for a moment. "But it's not really you, is it?"

"No," I said, "it's not."

"Early June Allyson," he decided, looking at the four-poster bed and the dressing table with the perfume bottles. "Early Gloria DeHaven." He sat down on the bed. "I've had such a nice evening. I hope you'll ask me again."

I gazed at him, at his bleached hair and bright blue eyes, at his surprisingly masculine hands, and wondered what was happening to me. I mean, I liked him so very much. And I didn't know why.

"You know, Heidi," he said after a minute, "you haven't told me anything about yourself. We've only talked about me."

"What would you like to know?"

"Everything."

I sat down on the bed. "It's complicated."

"Try me," he suggested.

"You wouldn't understand."

"Try me," he said again.

"OK!" I burst out. "If you want to know the truth, I'm a complete and total failure. I don't have beauty or talent, or personality or brains, and nobody on this earth finds me interesting. I don't stand out in any way. My life is a bust. There's nothing wonderful about me, Jeffrey."

"But you are!" he exclaimed, grabbing my hand. "You *are* wonderful! I knew it the minute I looked at you, the minute I saw that fabulous coat and chic little haircut. You *are* wonderful, Heidi. That's why I let you pick me up."

"I picked you up?"

"Of course you did! How old are you, sweetie? Sixteen, seventeen?"

"Sixteen."

"Right, and that's still very young, isn't it? What do you want to be later on? Do you know?"

"A bicycle messenger. A car shepherd."

Jeffrey laughed. "Come on now!"

"A massage therapist?" I suggested.

Jeffrey squeezed my hand. "Don't worry about it. Because whatever you're going to be is inside you right now, this minute, and it always has been. You were born you, just as I was born me, and if you believe in yourself nothing can go wrong. Why are you so hard on yourself?"

"I don't know."

"What's your father like?"

I was surprised by this question. "Well, he's quite nice—except that he wants me to be Albert Einstein. And *she* wants me to be Marilyn Monroe. They're divorced."

"Yes, I assumed that. But you know, Heidi, I liked your mother, I really did. She's sort of an ethnic Bette Davis."

"No kidding? Is that the way you see her?"

"Oh my, yes! She's stylized. But lots of fun."

I tried to think of Shirley as being lots of fun, and failed. "We don't get along too well. Our values are different."

"May I?" asked Jeffrey, lying back on the bed. "You know, for as long as I can remember, I wanted to bleach my hair and wear makeup. But I was afraid of what people would think. Then, two years ago, I said to myself, Jeffrey, life is short. If you want to wear makeup, do it! And if you want to go around in drag, do that too. It doesn't matter what people think of you—it only matters what you think of yourself."

"Does Sister Margaret know you're gay?"

"Yes. She does."

"You *told* her, Jeffrey?"

"Of course."

And then there was a pause.

"So you think I'm not a total washout," I said after a few minutes.

63

He looked at me. "Heidi, we've only known each other a short time, but I think you're an original. I knew it the minute I saw your coat."

"My mother hates that coat."

"I know, I know, most mothers would. But my dear, it has such class! Whoever it belonged to was someone special."

"I think so too."

Jeffrey was gazing at me as though he wanted to figure me out. "Tell me something you've never told anyone else," he said. "Something private."

I laughed. "Well . . . that's hard. You first."

"OK. I wanted to be a priest when I was little."

"A priest?"

"Yes. It seemed like the solution to everything."

I cast around in my mind for something to tell him. "I . . . I'm lonely," I said. "I don't fit in anywhere."

"I knew that already."

Jeffrey closed his eyes and began to hum to himself, and I just sat there—amazed by the things we had said to each other. I felt very excited and very sad. Simultaneously.

"I don't want to overstay my welcome," said Jeffrey, glancing at his watch. "Will you walk me to the door?"

We walked into the foyer and stood there looking at each other. "Will you say good-night to your mother for me?" Jeffrey asked. "And thank her for a wonderful evening?"

"Yes. Of course."

"Well then, Heidi, good night."

"Jeffrey—may I come and watch you dance tomorrow night? In front of the theater?"

He smiled. "Of course. Tomorrow I'll be at the Broadhurst. Do you know where that is?"

"I'll find it."

He kissed my cheek. "Good night then, Heidi dear."

"Good night."

The minute the door closed, Shirley called to me from her bedroom. I had hoped she was asleep, but her voice was like a sergeant's. "Heidi!" she demanded. "Come in here."

I went into her bedroom, closing the door behind me. Shirley was wearing a satin nightgown and a bed jacket. Her hair was in rollers and she still had on her pearls. She was reading *TV Guide.* "Is he gone?" she asked.

"You know he's gone. You heard the door close. Mother—didn't you like him at all?"

Shirley took off her reading glasses and perused me. "Baby, you must be out of your mind to make friends with someone like that. But I guess it's your age. You'll just have to chalk it up to experience."

"What?"

"Chalk it up to experience. Because he is not coming here again."

"Jeffrey is my friend. I will see him whenever I want to."

"No," said Shirley, "you won't. Heidi, these people have *diseases*, don't you know that? I'll have to get rid of all the dishes he used."

"I hate you," I said softly. And then I left the room.

9

Three days later I was sitting on a bench by the East River. It was a cold gray day, and I had forgotten to wear my seaman's cap, but I did not feel the cold. All I could think of was Jeffrey and the hours we had spent together on Saturday night. All I could feel was his hand in mine as we walked up Eighth Avenue.

I had told Shirley that I was going to the movies with some kids from school, and by seven-thirty I was standing in front of the Broadhurst Theater. Jeffrey was there, on the sidewalk, dancing to the tape recorder. It was playing a tune called "Get Happy" and Judy Garland was singing it.

"Forget your troubles, c'mon get happy," sang Judy—and as she sang, Jeffrey did a slow, lazy wonderful tap dance. His eyes were closed and he had a little smile on his face.

People put coins in his hat. Curtain time approached and more people went into the theater. Jeffrey winked at me and kept on dancing. A lady in a mink coat gave him two dollars. Then everyone disappeared inside and the sidewalk was empty. "Let's go somewhere for dinner!" Jeffrey said gaily. "My treat."

We walked over to a Howard Johnson's on Eighth Avenue and took a table near the window. Jeffrey obviously had money tonight, because he ordered us both hamburger platters and malteds. And the minute the order was placed, we started to talk. It was as though we had been waiting our whole lives to meet one another, and now that we had, we couldn't stop talking.

"How many foster homes were you in?" I asked, as our food arrived.

"Two," said Jeffrey. "One when I was a baby, and another in my teens. In between, from the ages of eight to twelve, I was in the orphanage." He grinned. "Dancing my head off."

"When did you realize that you were talented?"

"Around the age of five. Every time I heard music, I danced. I just couldn't stop dancing."

"What's your singing voice like, Jeffrey?"

By way of demonstration, he stopped eating and sang a few bars of an old tune called "Pennies from Heaven." His voice was beautiful.

"Were you ever in a real show?" I asked.

"Only in high school, and you know what *those* productions are like. We did Gilbert and Sullivan every spring. . . . You know, Heidi, you have a funny way of concentrating on me, when I want to concentrate on *you*. It's your turn now. Do you have a boyfriend?"

I felt myself blushing. "No."

"A special girlfriend?"

"No. I did have one, Veronica Bangs, but she moved away."

"Then who do you share things with?"

You, I wanted to say—you, from now on. But I didn't. "Jeffrey?" I said, "have you ever been in love?"

That strange little look of sadness I had seen before crossed his face. "Yes," he replied. "Once."

"Do you have a . . . a friend? You know what I mean."

"No," he said. "I'm quite alone now."

It was the "now" that got to me, as though he had once been deeply involved—but as though something tragic had happened. "Is it OK for me to ask you these things?"

He took my hand, turned it over and kissed it. "You can ask me anything you like. You're my friend."

We each had a second cup of coffee, and then we walked out into the cold night. There was a traffic jam on Eighth Avenue and horns were blaring.

Above the noisy city, the stars glittered. "Show me where you live," I said to Jeffrey. "I'd like to see it."

He was shivering, the collar of his fur jacket pulled up around his neck. "You don't want to see where I live, Heidi."

"Yes, I do. It's important to me."

So we walked over to 53rd Street, holding hands, and headed west. "You're not going to like this," said Jeffrey. "It's sordid."

Well, all right. I had thought I was prepared to see where he slept every night, but I wasn't. Because it was an abandoned brownstone near the river, with boarded-up windows, and garbage all over the sidewalk. In an apartment on the second floor of this building, five people had set up housekeeping.

It was so terrible. Mattresses on the floor and people sleeping with piles of blankets on top of them. One man had a Sterno burner and was making soup. Another person, a woman, who was wrapped in many layers of clothes, had a cat curled up with her. Just mattresses, and dirty blankets, and candles in wine bottles. People's possessions in heaps on the floor. No electricity and no water. A smell of despair.

Jeffrey led me back outdoors, where the fresh air was a relief. We sat down on the front steps together. "Who are they?" I said.

He smiled his sad little smile. "Just people. People like me, who have no money and no homes. One of those men up there was a lawyer, would you believe

70

it? But he became an alcoholic and now he begs on the street. The woman with the cat is crazy. Her name is Annie."

"They keep talking about the homeless on television . . ."

"I know," he said gently, "but it's never quite real, is it?"

"How do they get food? Or baths, or anything?"

"At the various churches and shelters. I myself prefer the Salvation Army, downtown."

"But why don't all of you sleep in the shelters?"

"Because it's dangerous, love. People attack you."

I shook my head. "Jeffrey, this just isn't right. You can't live this way."

"What would you suggest?"

"I'll think of something," I said angrily. "I mean, my God, you're a talented performer!"

So now I was sitting by the East River with a heart as heavy as lead. Planes were taking off from La Guardia Airport, streaking through the cold gray sky. Nursemaids pushed babies in shiny carriages. Women in expensive coats walked their dogs.

I thought of Peter Applebaum, the person on whom I once had a terrible crush, and then I thought of Pablo Gonzalez, who used to deliver our groceries. I had been in love with Pablo when I was twelve years old, but was that really love? Was Peter Applebaum *love*? No. Not in any way. But now I, Heidi

Rosenbloom, was finally in love and the feeling was not altogether wonderful. The feeling, as a matter of fact, was very close to pain—a tight little pain around the heart that would not go away. And it didn't matter that Jeffrey was twenty years old, and gay, and a street person. I loved him.

In three days it would be Christmas, and what would Jeffrey do then? Celebrate in his crumbling brownstone with alcoholics and crazy people? Have a meal at the Salvation Army? Dance in front of a theater as people in mink coats swept by, dropping a few coins in his hat?

I walked home at a brisk pace, hoping that Shirley would be at the hairdresser's, and she was. The apartment was empty. So the first thing I did was rummage around in my desk drawer until I located my bank book. I had a savings account that Leonard added to on birthdays and holidays, and in this account was exactly four hundred dollars. Was four hundred enough to get Jeffrey a hotel room? I phoned the Meridian, a cheap hotel on 33rd Street, and learned that their rooms cost fifty dollars a night. In other words, three hundred and fifty a week.

Well then, I would give Jeffrey the four hundred and let him do what he wanted with it. At least it would buy him food and a winter coat. I would put the money in a Christmas card and tie a small teddy bear around the card with a ribbon.

I took off That Coat and ran a hand over my crew cut. What to do next? Call Veronica, said a voice in my head, and get some advice. People always say that Veronica is sixteen years old going on sixty.

It was noon in New York, and nine o'clock in Los Angeles. Her phone rang for a long time and then she answered it. "Heidi?" she said. "You should have called after five. It's cheaper."

"I know, but I have to talk to you. Something has happened."

"Don't tell me," she said. "Let me guess. You were expelled."

"No. Of course not. Why would I be expelled?"

"Just kidding, old girl. Let me try again. You lost your virginity."

"No," I said sadly, "I didn't. And anyway, we were going to send telegrams when that happened."

"Your mother's getting married again?"

"*No*, Veronica."

"I've got it!" she said. "You're in love."

I was very surprised. Because since Veronica had moved away our relationship had suffered. Until a year ago we had been able to read each other's minds and finish each other's sentences. But distance had changed all that.

"Well . . . yes," I said. "In a way."

"Terrific! Does he go to Spencer? What grade is he in? Is he gorgeous?"

Suddenly I realized that it wasn't going to be easy to talk about this. "Uh, he's older than we are," I began. "Twenty."

"Super. Is he in college?"

"Not exactly."

"So what does he do?"

"Well . . . he's in the theater. He's a dancer."

"Neat," said Veronica. "What show is he in?"

Something told me that I should either tell her the truth, the whole truth, or end the conversation. "He's not in any show," I said. "He's dancing in the street so he can be discovered. He's gay."

There was a silence on the other end of the phone, and it was not a comfortable one. "God," said Veronica at last.

"I know. It's difficult."

"*Difficult?* Are you out of your mind? He's probably got AIDS or something."

"Don't be ridiculous!"

"Heidi, look. You've probably never known any gay men before, but I have. Two of them. And they're terrible. I mean, they go to bars and pick each other up and everything."

"Jeffrey's not like that at all. The only odd thing about him is that he bleaches his hair."

"Oh, no!" she groaned. "A drag queen. Heidi, are you out of your mind?"

"He's very gentle," I said. "He grew up in an orphanage."

"For God's sake, come to your senses! There's nothing in this for you."

"I . . . I don't know. I think it's too soon to tell."

"Lord!" she said. "With all the eligible boys in New York, you have to go and find someone gay. You always do things the hardest way possible, don't you?"

Disappointment was washing over me, so I said, "I have to go now, Veronica. This call is expensive."

"Heidi, come to your senses. There's nothing *in it* for you. And anyway . . ."

But I had already hung up the phone.

10

On Christmas morning I woke up so depressed that I could hardly get out of bed. It was snowing again, and all I could think of was Jeffrey—lying on his mattress in that awful building. What was life all about when Shirley and I, and her best friend Bobo Lewis, were waking up in a warm and comfortable apartment while other people were suffering?

Bobo Lewis, who was a widow who lived in Westchester, had been spending Christmases with us since her husband Alfred died. She was a fat, cheerful woman who was always trying to diet, and while I didn't dislike her, she was not the company I might have chosen for Christmas Day. But it didn't matter, because Jeffrey and I had arranged to meet at Danny's Coffee Shop at six P.M. My father, who was supposed to come over to Shirley's for Christmas dinner, had the flu.

I had worked out this day very carefully, because I wanted to give Jeffrey the best Christmas of his life. Most of his Christmases, he told me, had been difficult, and the day was a hard one for him. So what I had planned was to open presents with Bobo and Shirley, have Christmas dinner with them, zip downtown to Leonard's apartment and give him *his* present, and then arrive at Danny's Coffee Shop at six. I had put Jeffrey's money into a beautiful Christmas card and had tied a very small teddy bear around it with a piece of red wool.

It was seven A.M. and I needed a cup of coffee, so I opened my door and began to tiptoe through the living room. Shirley's Christmas tree—white, with silver ornaments—stood near the piano, glowing weirdly in the gloom. For one minute I saw myself at the age of six sitting by the tree watching an electric train go round and round. I was hugging a doll and Leonard and Shirley were laughing.

I made a cup of instant coffee and tiptoed back towards my bedroom. But I was not to complete the journey because Bobo, an early riser, intercepted me. She was standing in the living room gazing at the tree, and she was wearing a red quilted bathrobe that made her look huge. "Heidi!" she exclaimed. "Merry Christmas!"

"Thank you," I said. "Merry Christmas to you, too."

Bobo came over and kissed me, almost spilling my coffee. "Merry Christmas, baby doll. I bet you can't wait to open your presents."

"Right," I said. "Right."

"I got your mother something *fantastic*," Bobo said in an exaggerated whisper. "Wait till you see it."

She went off to the kitchen to make herself a cup of tea, and I hurried back to my room. What Jeffrey didn't know was that Christmas was a hard day for me, too, one of the worst, and that last Christmas I had drunk half a bottle of sherry just to get through the whole thing. And why? Because Leonard had arrived, as usual, with champagne and presents, only to get into a fight with Shirley. It happened every year. A turkey, presents, carols on the stereo, and then—bang—some sort of blowup. One Christmas he had even taken the tree, trimmed and lighted, and thrown it out of the window. Yet the two of them insisted that we all spend holidays together because, as Shirley put it, we were "still a family."

I sat by my bedroom window looking out at the snow, trying to remember that six-year-old who had been given an electric train. I turned on my radio and listened to some carols. Then I closed my eyes and said, "Merry Christmas, Jeffrey."

By nine A.M. Shirley was in the kitchen, making coffee and warming croissants. Then she and Bobo

78

and I—still in our bathrobes—sat by the white-and-silver tree and began to open presents. Bobo had given my mother a huge heating pad from Bloomingdale's that also gave you a massage—and Shirley had given her something called The Stomach Eliminator, a portable fitness machine. For me, Bobo had chosen a set of classics meant for very small children, and so I sat there holding copies of *Black Beauty* and *Pinocchio* on my lap. "Gee," I said, "thank you."

I had given Shirley an assortment of cast albums from Broadway shows, and she seemed pleased with them. But when I opened my presents from her, my heart sank. Shirley had bought me 1) some lace underwear, made in France 2) a traveling makeup kit, stocked with all kinds of eye shadow, lipsticks, and blushers 3) two shortie cotton nightgowns and 4) an assortment of bangle bracelets. "The bracelets are Calvin Klein," she said. "I saw them in Saks just two days ago."

"Adorable," said Bobo. "Really cute."

"Yeah," I said falsely, "they are. Thank you, Mom."

"The makeup kit you could take *anywhere*," Shirley explained.

"It's true," said Bobo. "You could take it anywhere. It's adorable."

"I'm going to take a bath now," I said with false cheerfulness. "See you gals later."

We ate Christmas dinner at two o'clock. And there was enough food for an army. Turkey with all the trimmings, and lots of vegetables, and a big salad. For dessert, Shirley had bought pies at a fancy bakery on Madison Avenue.

"Happy holidays!" said Shirley, raising her glass of wine. "Here's to all of us."

"Right!" said Bobo. "Good health." We all clinked glasses.

Shirley and Bobo were dressed up—in afternoon dresses and jewelry—while I was in jeans and a turtleneck sweater. "You're not going down to your father's that way?" Shirley asked me. "On Christmas?"

"Yep," I said. "I am."

"Sweetie," said Bobo, her mouth full of turkey, "why don't you dress up a little today? To please Mama."

"I like the way I look," I declared, "and this is what I'm wearing. Anyway, Daddy never notices what I wear."

"You shouldn't let that influence you," said Shirley. "Just because he's a slob, doesn't mean you have to be one."

"Ah Mom, please . . ."

"He's such a slob," Shirley said to Bobo, who was chewing with her mouth open.

"He's not coming today?" asked Bobo, who knew very well that he wasn't.

"Flu," said Shirley. "I don't even know that Heidi should be around him. He's probably contagious."

Shirley was serving up the pie now, apple and mince, and there was also whipped cream to put on the top. "I don't want any dessert," I said, rising to my feet. "Will you excuse me?"

Bobo had taken both kinds of pie, and was heaping her plate with gobs of the cream. "Heidi, sweetheart, you have *got* to taste this pie. It looks dreamy."

"Come on, baby, at least have a piece of pie," said my mother. "You've been eating like a bird."

"Like a little sparrow!" echoed Bobo. "Like a robin!"

"I'll see you later," I said.

Feeling sick to my stomach, I went into my room, put my father's present and Jeffrey's present into a duffel bag, and marched back through the living room. "Don't wear that awful coat!" my mother called from the dining room. "Wear your good one!"

"Right," I called back, as I put on That Coat and my wool seaman's cap. "I'll see you later."

"How late will you be?" yelled Shirley. "It's snowing out there."

"After I see Daddy, I'm going to meet some friends for coffee. Don't worry about me."

I got out of there rapidly, and went down in the elevator with a fat man who was smoking a cigar.

When I hit the street, the snow was coming down thick and fast.

There weren't many people on Lexington Avenue, and the lighted store windows looked pretty through the swirling snow. I hailed a cab and settled back against the worn leather seat. "The Village," I said to the driver. "West 13th Street."

He turned around and stared at me. "Merry Christmas," he said reprovingly.

I stared back and saw that he was dressed like Santa Claus, from head to toe. "Right," I said. "Merry Christmas. Excuse me."

11

My father was propped up in bed with a thermometer in his mouth, and his one-room apartment was a mess. Clothes, books, and magazines all over the place. Dirty ashtrays, used coffee cups. "I'm sorry you caught the flu," I said to him, taking off my coat.

"Don't come too close," he said weakly. "It's catching."

I hung up my coat in the hall closet, took his present out of my duffel bag, and sat down on a chair at a safe distance. "It's too bad," I said. "On Christmas and everything."

"So how's your mother?" he asked. "Did she go overboard again?"

I knew that he was talking about presents. "No, no, she didn't spend much. And Bobo's there."

He groaned. "*That* moron? I'm glad I got sick."

"Bobo comes every Christmas, Daddy, you know that."

"I know, I know. . . . You'd think she would have remarried by now. She's got a few million."

"Dollars?" I asked.

"How your mother can stand that fatty, I'll never know. It revolts me just to look at her."

"Daddy," I said, "it's Christmas. Let's not talk this way."

"All right, all right. What did your mother give you?"

"Just some stuff to wear. Would you like me to fix you some soup? You look pretty ill."

"I don't need anything. Go get your presents, pussycat. They're on my desk."

I went over to Leonard's rolltop desk and retrieved my presents. One was a check for a hundred dollars, and the other was a pair of pink earmuffs.

"Pretty cute, huh?" he said, referring to the earmuffs. "Put them on, baby. Let's see how you look."

I put on the earmuffs. They looked terrible.

Leonard opened his present from me, which was a cashmere scarf from Brooks Brothers, his favorite store. "Well, well," he said. "Nothing too good for the old man, eh?"

He put the scarf around his neck and perused the thermometer. "This thing must be haywire. It doesn't even show that I have a temperature. And I know that I have one because I'm so hot."

"Have you seen a doctor?" I asked. I was still on the other side of the room.

"No, it isn't that bad. So did your mother cook a meal, or what? Sometimes she orders it from that place over on First Avenue."

"She cooked it from scratch. Oh Daddy, I should have brought you some!"

"It's not important," he said. "What are the girls going to do today? Go out or something?"

"I don't think so. They'll just stay around the house."

"And what about my baby? What is *she* going to do?"

"I'm meeting some kids from school," I said brightly. "Uptown, for coffee."

"Nice kids at that school. Well-bred. Polite."

I thought of the types who went to Spencer, and shuddered. "It's true," I said.

Leonard sighed. "I got a notice from your building that it may be going co-op. Did you know that? Does your mother know it?"

"We haven't heard a word about it."

"Well, you can tell Shirley that I'm not buying that apartment for her. You, my baby, will be off to college in two years, so your mother should be thinking of moving to a smaller place anyway. I'm not a millionaire."

"Daddy," I said, "it's Christmas."

"Hmmm?" he answered. "Honey, would you go

into the kitchen and pour me some juice? My mouth is dry."

I poured him some juice, found the aspirin bottle, and put some Campbell's soup on the stove. As I stirred the soup, I had an overwhelming desire to tell him about Jeffrey—which of course would have been a disaster. I mean, my father is very sensitive about effeminate men and uses the word "fairy" a lot. He once had an office boy named Harold Brodie, who was very handsome and polite, and so he decided that Harold was a fairy. "He comes into my office in the morning and I think he's going to kiss me!" Leonard had said. "He's all twinkles and smiles."

Harold had lasted for one month and then Leonard had replaced him with a little thug named Mickey Malone who eventually stole a diamond watch from Leonard's desk and was arrested. But—would you believe it—it was Mickey who Leonard remembered with affection, not Harold. No, I decided, Jeffrey would have to remain a secret.

By five-thirty the snow had stopped and I was racing uptown in another taxi. I felt badly about Leonard's lonely Christmas, but at the same time it was a relief to get away from him. I looked out the cab window and saw streets that were almost deserted. Everyone was indoors, having Christmas dinner. The snow was still white and clean.

As the cab pulled up in front of Danny's Coffee Shop, my heart began to pound. Jeffrey was sitting at a table near the window and waved at me. And as I entered the coffee shop he came up and wrapped his arms around me. "Merry Christmas, Heidi!"

"Merry Christmas," I said, my face buried in his fur jacket.

And suddenly it *was* Christmas, and everything was beautiful—the red-and-green tablecloths on the little tables, and the room decorated with pine boughs, and a wonderful smell of cooking in the air. The coffee shop felt safe, and lovely, and warm.

"Did you dance today?" I asked Jeffrey, as he helped me off with my coat.

"No," he said, "I took the day off. Went to Rockefeller Center and watched people ice skate. It was lovely."

"I'm so glad to see you."

We gazed at each other. Jeffrey had a sprig of holly pinned to his jacket. His cheeks were rosy.

He had ordered dinner for us—a turkey special for $10.95, complete with coffee and dessert—and I enjoyed every bite of it. "This is so much better than what we had at home," I said. "It's delicious."

He was holding my hand with his left hand, and eating with his right. "I have a present for you, Heidi."

"Me too," I said, studying him. His eyes were as blue as blue marbles, the kind I had played with as a child.

When the waiter had cleared our plates away and brought coffee, Jeffrey reached into the back pocket of his jeans. "I don't know if you'll like this. It's a rather odd gift."

"I would like anything you gave me."

He shook his head in a funny way, and handed me a tiny white box, the kind you can get in any dime store. "Well, open it, love. Don't be shy."

But I hesitated. Because I wanted so terribly to like whatever he had gotten me, wanted so terribly to appreciate it.

I opened the box and found a little gold cross inside—on a chain. It was very simple and I could tell that it was old. "Oh, Jeffrey . . ."

"I know you're Jewish, love, but it's the only nice thing I own. Sister gave it to me for my twelfth birthday."

"Sister Margaret gave you this?"

"Yes, and since it's always given me comfort, I want you to have it now."

"But Jeffrey, I don't need comfort!"

"Yes," he said softly. "You do."

I put the cross around my neck and went over to a mirror that was near the cash register. "It looks beautiful," I said, returning to the table. "But how can I take something that . . ."

"Shh," he said, putting his hand over my mouth.

Suddenly I knew that my present for him was not right. Because compared to that little gold cross, four one-hundred-dollar bills was vulgar—something that Leonard might have thought of, not me. Yet there was nothing I could do about it now. I handed Jeffrey the Christmas card with the teddy bear tied to it.

"I'm *mad* about this bear," said Jeffrey. "What's his name?"

"Woody Allen," I replied. And we laughed.

Jeffrey untied the red wool and opened his Christmas card. There was a poem printed on it, about friendship and holidays, and all that, and Jeffrey read the words carefully. Then he looked at the money. His mouth twitched ever so slightly and I could tell that he was moved. "Heidi—this is the most generous thing that anyone's ever done for me, but you know something? I'm not going to take it now. Keep it for me, and if I ever need it, if I'm ever desperate, then I'll ask you."

But you're desperate now! I wanted to say. You live with bums and crazy people, and half the time you don't get enough to eat. But instead, I said, "OK. If that's what you want."

"It is, love. But I *will* keep Woody. He's adorable."

He handed the money back to me and I put it in my pocket. Then Jeffrey leaned across the table and kissed me. It was only a kiss on the cheek, but it was different from his hello/good-bye kisses. It was very tender.

"I wish I could have had you to the apartment today, Jeffrey. But this is nicer, isn't it?"

"It's all right, Heidi. I know that your mother doesn't like me."

I swallowed hard. "It isn't that."

"Don't worry about it. I know how I look to people. It's made clear to me every day."

I wanted to ask him questions. Why he dressed the way he did, if it was such a disadvantage, and why he was willing to live in poverty. I wanted to ask him who he had been in love with long ago, and if he could ever love me. But all I said was: "What shall we do now? Take a walk?"

His face lit up. "Let's go to church somewhere. I haven't been to church for ages."

"A Catholic church, you mean?"

"Any church. Let's walk till we find one."

So we walked out into the streets that were bright with snow, and headed west. Some little kids passed us, singing carols, and we waved at them.

Eighth Avenue, Ninth Avenue, and still we could not find a church. "There!" said Jeffrey. "Across the street."

It was called St. Andrew's and it was Catholic—and the doors were unlocked. But there was no one inside. Only an old lady in a pew near the altar, praying. From some distant place in the church the sound of an organ could be heard. "I haven't been to mass for five years," Jeffrey whispered.

I didn't know how to answer him. I just knew that we were walking down the aisle together, our footsteps echoing in the silence. The church was very large and very beautiful, with many candles burning. I sat down in the pew, but Jeffrey didn't. He knelt first, on a little bench, crossed himself, and said a prayer.

I could not tell where the organ music was coming from, it seemed so far away. And I could not tell whether or not Jeffrey was still praying. His head was bowed, but his eyes were open. He seemed at peace. And as the music continued, and as Jeffrey reached for my hand, I knew that what I felt was happiness. I had waited my whole life for this feeling without knowing what it was—and this was it.

12

On New Year's Eve I stood in front of my full-length mirror, studying myself. I had had my crew cut trimmed, and had purchased several new items from the thrift shop where I had bought That Coat. One of the items was a green tam-o'-shanter, which I was wearing on my head at the moment—and the other was a man's plaid vest. The vest, plus the tam, plus That Coat, made a very interesting outfit, which Jeffrey had been crazy about. On the spot, I had taken him in a taxi to the store, called Grandma's Attic, and bought him a heavy turtleneck sweater. It looked great with his fur jacket.

Jeffrey thinks I am original, I said to myself, as I stared into the mirror. Jeffrey thinks that I am even wonderful. Was it true, or was it simply that Jeffrey was an optimist? I didn't know, but I did have to admit that I liked my new look. It mitigated, if that is the right word, my shortness.

I was wearing Jeffrey's gold cross at all times, but kept it hidden under shirts and sweaters so that Shirley would not see it. She had not mentioned his name since the night of our dinner party, so I hadn't either. As far as she was concerned, he was gone, because Shirley had a way of making things disappear of which she did not approve. But she was very busy these days—with her social life, with her work for the Red Cross—all of which gave me the freedom I needed.

On the other hand, I had never lacked for freedom—owing to the fact that Shirley did not know what life was like in New York for a teenager. She did not know that one out of three private school kids get mugged before they hit the tenth grade, and she did not know that the gathering place for all of teenage New York—as far as drugs were concerned—was the Sheep Meadow in Central Park. She did not know that every girl in my class was on the Pill, and that one kid had actually been sent to a reformatory because of dealing crack. Both she and Leonard believed that I lived in a glass bubble.

All of which allowed me to see Jeffrey as much as I wanted to—which was every day. In the last week we had fallen into a pattern, in which I met him in the late afternoons in front of some theater, and we then went for dinner and a Broadway show. Yes, a show. Because Jeffrey had discovered that it is possible to get into a show for free by drifting in with the crowd after the first intermission. As the house lights go down, one quickly cases the joint. If there are spare seats in the auditorium, one hurries into them. If there aren't, one joins the standees at the back. This meant that Jeffrey and I never got to see the first act of any show, but what the hell. We had a great time seeing the second acts of musicals like *Big River* and *42nd Street.* Then we would go for coffee.

"I will be studying at Carol Cameron's house tonight," I would tell Shirley. "Home around eleven." Or: "Tonight my English class has its Russian novel evening. I'll be home late." Or: "Tammy Parish is having a party tonight. We're going to listen to records." The only problem being that Tammy Parish had moved to Australia with her parents a year ago.

In the past week Jeffrey had started going to open calls—auditions for plays and musicals to which anyone can come, but which are a very rough experience. I had been to one with him, at a Broadway theater, and had been depressed by it because there were hundreds of people there, just waiting for a chance to be seen. They were given cards with numbers on them, and when their number was called they got to do a few moments of something. A song, or a dance, or both. Sometimes the performer would only be on stage for a second when a voice would call from the darkened auditorium, "Thank you, dear, that's enough," and you'd know that he had not made it.

The musical that Jeffrey tried out for was called *Hurdy Gurdy* and it needed ten boys for the chorus. And when it was Jeffrey's turn up there, my heart went into my mouth. I was standing backstage with a lot of other people, but I had a good view of him—and he looked so small out on the stage, so vulnerable. He had asked the piano player to play "Get Happy" and then he had started in on his lazy, sweet, tap routine. But he was only one minute into the routine when the voice from the darkened theater came. "Thanks so much. That'll be all." Jeffrey's audition was over.

"It's all right," he said to me afterwards. "It's a way of getting my feet wet."

"But Jeffrey, don't you feel rejected?"

"Not at all," he replied. "It's part of the game."

There were so many things I wanted to ask him—as we prowled around the theater district, as we ate in coffee shops—so many questions about his past. But there was never time. Because either Jeffrey was dancing in front of theaters, or reading the trade papers, or going to open calls. He acted like he knew all the ropes—though he didn't—and the thing that got to me was that he was so full of hope. I mean, even *I* knew how hard it is to break into show business, yet the whole thing was as real to Jeffrey as though he was already a star.

"Why do you want it so much?" I asked him one day. We were standing in the back of an empty theater, watching the stage manager set up the stage for auditions.

Jeffrey looked at the darkened auditorium, with its plush seats and sloping aisles. He looked at the work light burning on stage and the brick wall at the back. "It's all that love," he replied, "all those people reaching out to you as you perform. And it's the feeling of *being* there, onstage. The lights are like broken rainbows, and you feel you're standing in a magic circle, and the silence of the audience—when you're good—is like the silence of God. Oh Heidi, don't you see? All that is worth everything."

"Jeffrey dear, how do you know? You've never even been in a play."

He turned and looked fiercely at me. "I know, Heidi. I *know*."

So I bought him new sweaters, and new jeans, and hung around theaters while he danced on the sidewalk. Sometimes people heckled him, or said unpleasant things like, "Get a job, kiddo, get a job," but none of it seemed to faze him. Jeffrey just kept on dancing.

And now it was New Year's Eve and I was studying myself in the mirror. I wouldn't be seeing Jeffrey tonight because New Year's was a busy time for him. People got drunk and were generous with their money, etc. Shirley was going to a party downstairs in our building, and I, of course, was going nowhere. Not *one person* in my class had invited me to any of the usual New Year's Eve parties, but I couldn't have cared less. What I intended to do was open a very small bottle of champagne for myself at midnight and toast Jeffrey. At that hour, he would probably be dancing in front of some fashionable restaurant like "21."

I sat down on my bed and thought about New Year's. Leonard was still in bed with the flu, so he would be alone, and Shirley was spending the evening with people she didn't even like—the Lowensteins. Long ago the three of us used to celebrate by going to Radio City Music Hall and seeing the stage show—and then Leonard would take us to Lindy's for a late supper. It was hard to believe, but we had been a family once. Shirley keeps all these photo albums, and there are dozens of pictures of the old days: Leonard and Shirley and Heidi on birthdays and holidays, on beaches and sailboats. For a while Leonard had had a big thing about "motor trips," and so we had gone to places like the Adirondacks and Bar Harbor, Maine. How, I asked myself, *how* was it possible that Jane Anne Mosley had ruined all this? She was a real nobody—despite her two published stories—and I hated her so much that I had once threatened her by telephone. Yes, it's true. At the age of thirteen I had phoned her from a booth on the street, using a phony German accent. "You vill pay for what you haff done," I said.

"What?" Jane Anne said in alarm. "Who is this?"

"You vill *pay* for what you haff done. Ve are all vatching you. You are beink followed!"

"Who *is* this, for God's sake?"

"Ze German mafia. We haff a contract on you, so beware!"

There had been a gasp on the other end of the phone and Jane Anne had hung up. But I had rattled her, if only for a few moments, and I was glad.

Would Leonard and Shirley ever get back together again? It would save on rent, and instead of fighting over the phone, they could fight in person. Did I want them to marry again? Yes. Because we were all so lonely now. It doesn't matter, I said to myself. You have Jeffrey.

As though the word "Jeffrey" had swept her into the room, Shirley entered. She was wearing a navy dress, and high heels, and her three strands of pearls. She surveyed my outfit of tam-o'-shanter, man's vest, and That Coat. "You're going to a costume party?" she asked.

"Of course not, Mom. Don't be silly."

"Then why are you wearing such clothes? You look like something out of vaudeville."

"Good," I said.

"Don't you want to come to the Lowenstein's party? They're dying for you to come."

98

"Mom, please. I don't like the Lowensteins. And neither do you."

"They specifically said, 'Bring that darling daughter of yours along. Bring Heidi.'"

"I'll bet."

"I think it's too bad, you sitting here alone. I wish you had a date."

"Mother, I have told you a thousand times, people don't date anymore. They go out in groups."

"Well, if you change your mind, just come down to the Lowensteins'. In some other clothes, of course."

"Of course," I said. "Of course."

"You could wear that red velvet dress. The one with the puffed sleeves."

"Right."

"And if you do come, baby, put on just a little lipstick. OK?"

"Absolutely," I said. "Happy New Year."

Shirley came over and kissed me on the cheek. "You too, baby. I'll look in on you when I come back."

As soon as I heard the front door close, I took off That Coat and my green tam-o'-shanter and put my tiny bottle of champagne into the fridge. Then I turned on the television to the cable news station. As befits any holiday, the news was all tragic. Ten people had died in a fire in the Bronx. There had been a massive car pileup on the Long Island Expressway. "And the homeless," said the announcer, "continue to suffer during this freezing holiday week. Our latest estimate is that there are ten thousand people seeking shelter tonight in the city of New York."

I put on my pajamas and an old wool bathrobe and curled up in front of the set. Where was Jeffrey at this moment? Dancing in front of Sardi's restaurant, dancing in front of the Winter Garden. With Judy singing her heart out on the tape recorder. With people throwing coins into his hat.

I must have fallen asleep, because when I woke it was ten minutes to twelve and the TV screen showed thousands of people gathered in Times Square, waiting for the ball to drop and a new year to begin. I rushed into the kitchen, got out my tiny bottle of champagne, and worked away at the cork. It was hard to get it loose, but slowly it began to give. Then the cork popped, and I poured myself a glass of the bubbly. As the ball dropped and the people in Times Square cheered, I raised my glass to Jeffrey. "Happy New Year," I said.

The phone rang.

Spilling some of the champagne, I raced into the hall and picked up the receiver. "Happy New Year!" said a familiar voice.

"*Jeffrey?* Is that you?"

"None other, darling. Happy New Year."

"Oh Jeffrey, where are you? I was just toasting you with a glass of champagne."

"I'm in a phone booth near the Helen Hayes Theater. I made *scads* of money tonight. The streets are brilliant."

"I wish we were together."

"Me too, me too!"

And that's when I lost my head, because I said into the phone, "Jeffrey? I love you."

But it was obvious that he didn't understand what I meant. "I love you too, dearest! Listen, I've got to go. Other people are waiting to use this phone."

Carefully, I put down the phone. And then I went back to the living room, to watch the merrymakers on TV.

13

All too soon, Christmas vacation was over and I was back in the depressing atmosphere of The Spencer School. When I say depressing, I do not mean that Spencer was physically depressing—because physically it was a very good "plant," as Mr. Kaufman, the principal, always said: a brick building with many classrooms, many labs, a large auditorium, and an indoor swimming pool on the roof. No. Spencer depressed me because everyone there hung out in cliques, and I had never been in a clique. There were the hoods, the jocks, the brains, and the arty types—and I fit in with none of them.

However. I had Jeffrey now, and the fact that he was a part of my life made everything different. I would sit in class and finger the little gold cross around my neck and know that Jeffrey had given it to me. I would stare out the window during Algebra III and know that I would be meeting Jeffrey that night. The very fact that Jeffrey existed had changed the world for me—because at last I had someone to share things with. I mean, who had I been communicating with for the past twelve months? Taxi drivers. Policemen. Salesladies in stores.

Every week Leonard would ask me how I was doing in school and I would say, Fine, fine. He would ask me when I would be applying to college and I would say, Next year, Daddy, be patient. His choice for me was Radcliffe—which was so sad and so ridiculous that I couldn't even comment on it. Me, at Radcliffe? I had a C average.

Then a miracle occurred. A miracle that came out of the blue and took me totally by surprise. Shirley announced that Bobo Lewis was going to have her "bridge evenings" again, on Friday nights. Shirley would take the train up to Scarsdale every Friday and sleep over.

"Do you mind being left alone on Fridays?" she asked me. "If you mind, I won't go. I'll just tell Bobo that you hate being alone."

"Mom," I said, "please. *Go.* It will do you good."

My heart racing with excitement, I retreated to my room to make plans. Would Jeffrey be willing to sleep over on Friday nights? Of course. A warm bed in a warm apartment, good food and a glass of sherry. Without Shirley knowing it, I put clean sheets on the bed in the guest room and opened the windows one afternoon to air the place out. The guest room had once been Leonard's den.

At first, Jeffrey had reservations about the idea—and his cautiousness surprised me. Suppose my mother found out? Suppose the elevator man mentioned him? And was it nice in the first place to deceive Shirley that way? *Nice?* I thought. Nice doesn't even come into it.

And so he arrived that first Friday, bearing his tap shoes and tape recorder, and a book on the Broadway musical theater that he had bought in a second-hand book store. I took him into the guest room and his eyes widened. "Deluxe!" he exclaimed. "Super deluxe!"

"You can come every Friday, Jeffrey. And have a hot bath and a good meal."

He hugged me. "Oh Heidi, you're so terrific. What would I do without you?"

While I fixed my carefully planned dinner, Jeffrey wandered around the apartment, reading the titles of the books in the bookcase, studying the paintings, trying out the piano. "How wonderful it must be to live with beautiful things," he said, drifting into the kitchen. "On a daily basis, that is."

As he drifted out again, I realized that I had never been conscious of living with anything beautiful. Yet every single thing in the apartment made Jeffrey swoon. The rugs, the paintings, Shirley's antique love seat. The silver service on the sideboard in the dining room. The real Tiffany lamp.

"Dinner is ready," I announced—and Jeffrey and I walked into the dining room. He held my chair for me and I said thank you. We sat down and smiled at each other.

I am not the most wonderful cook in the world, but Jeffrey seemed to love the things I had made for him: roast chicken with potatoes, string beans, Parker House rolls. For dessert I had bought a cherry pie at Shirley's expensive bakery. We had coffee and after-dinner mints. Then we went into the living room. "What would you like to do now?" I asked.

Jeffrey looked shy. "Would it be . . . rude if I took a hot bath? I've been longing for one for days."

"Of course not! I'll run you one in Mom's bathtub. It's huge."

I went into Shirley's bathroom, poured a packet of bubble bath into the tub, and turned on the hot water. Jeffrey wandered in and stared at the over-sized tub and the marble sink. The glass dressing table. The indirect lighting. *"Divine,"* he said. "Do you have a bathrobe or something that I could wear?"

I handed him Shirley's peach satin robe. "How about this?"

He giggled. "Super. It's just my type."

I left him alone to soak in the tub, and as I put the dishes into the dishwasher I couldn't get over how natural it all seemed. Me cooking dinner for Jeffrey. Jeffrey taking a bubble bath. I had never felt so at home with another human being. He was like another self.

"You can come in if you like!" he called. "I am protected by bubbles!"

So I went into the bathroom and sat down on the closed toilet seat while Jeffrey luxuriated. "You cannot imagine how wonderful this is! Like dying and going to heaven."

"You will come here every Friday night," I said firmly, "and have a bubble bath. And a good dinner. And a soft bed."

"How dear you are, Heidi. How kind."

I looked at his naked shoulders, and turned away. When I turned back, Jeffrey had his eyes closed and had sunk farther down in the water. "This is so peaceful."

"I'll turn down your bed," I said to him.

It was only nine o'clock, but I had begun to realize how tired Jeffrey was. He never got enough sleep because his roommates, as he called them, kept him awake half the night by moaning and talking. And some nights it was too cold to sleep, too cold to do anything.

I turned down his bed and put his book on the Broadway musical theater on the night table. I brought in a glass of water, too. Then I switched on the little lamp by the bed and waited. In a few moments, Jeffrey came in. "I don't have any pajamas for you," I said apologetically.

"That's all right, love. I'll do without." He stretched out on the bed. "How lovely this is. How soft."

He was still wearing Shirley's satin robe, but had no self-consciousness about it. I put a mohair blanket over his legs. "I guess I should leave you now."

Jeffrey took my hand. "No, don't leave yet. Let's talk for a while."

"But aren't you tired?"

"No. Just relaxed."

I sat down on the side of the bed and gazed at him. He looked so young—sixteen or seventeen, maybe—and his eyes were very blue. My heart was pounding, the way it always did when I was near him. Let the right thing happen, I prayed. Please.

"Jeffrey," I said, "if you could do anything in the world you wanted, what would it be?"

"I'd find my mother," he replied.

This statement surprised me so much that I didn't know how to reply. "Are there ways of doing that?" I asked finally.

"I don't know. There must be. It's just that I haven't had the courage to try. . . . And what about you, Heidi? What do you want most in the world?"

To have you love me, I thought. But aloud, I said, "I don't know. To find out who I am, I guess."

"I've told you, dearest. Who you are is inside you

right now. You were born you—a totally unique and charming person."

I didn't mean to laugh, but it was a bitter little laugh that came out. "Jeffrey, in my whole life, nobody has ever found me charming. Or unique."

"I do. Isn't that enough?"

"Yes," I replied. And then there was a silence.

As the silence continued, and as Jeffrey closed his eyes, I realized that if I ever wanted to ask him things about himself, now was the time. This was a special moment we were having, and it might never come again. And so, taking a big risk, I said, "Jeffrey? What's it like to be gay?"

He opened his eyes. "I don't know, love. What's it like to be straight?"

"Touché."

"Touché indeed. What is it you really want to know?"

"Well . . . a lot of things."

"Such as?"

"Such as, did you always know about yourself?"

"Always. From the time I was little."

"And do you think you were born gay?"

"Yes."

"And are all gay men . . ." I stopped, unable to find the right word.

"Effeminate? No, of course not. Many are quite masculine."

"How many kinds of gay people are there?"

He winked at me. "How many kinds of straight people are there?"

"Thousands, I guess."

"Well—there you have it."

I was growing more and more confused, but I needed to go on with the conversation because I needed to understand him. "Most people think that gay people are strange," I said cautiously.

"Look," Jeffrey said, "the gay world is only a mirror-image of the straight world. And once you understand that, dear, nothing will seem strange. Gay men are doctors and lawyers and politicians—and street people—and some are promiscuous, and some aren't, and some have only one partner while others have many. The fact that I, my love, like to wear a little makeup from time to time is simply *me*."

"Jeffrey—will you take me to a gay bar?"

He looked shocked. "Absolutely not. Why would you ask me such a thing?"

"Well . . . because I want to understand you."

"Heidi dear, not even *I* go to gay bars anymore. And you do understand me. Just as I understand you."

I had crossed some kind of invisible line now, and could not retreat. "Do you have lovers?" I asked.

"No. Not at the moment."

"And who is the person who meant so much to you?"

That sad little smile—the one that always broke my heart—crossed Jeffrey's face. "His name was David. He died in a car accident."

"I . . . I'm sorry."

"No reason to be. It happened three years ago. I'm recovering."

"Are you scared about AIDS?" I said. At last—it had come out.

Jeffrey scanned my face for a moment. "Yes. I am scared as hell. We all are."

It was the "all" that hurt me—as though Jeffrey belonged to a world that I could never enter. A special club.

"Do you mind my talking about this?"

He yawned. "No darling, I don't. But I'm getting sleepy now. That bath was so hot."

I kissed him quickly on the cheek, and rose to my feet. "I hope you sleep well."

Jeffrey was gazing at me, holding my eyes with his. "Heidi? Will you remember something for me? For as long as you live?"

"Yes. Yes, Jeffrey. I will."

"Just remember that there is nothing you cannot accomplish in this world, if you want to badly enough. Sister used to say that to me over and over. And she was right."

"I'll remember that."

"Promise?"

"Yes."

"Then good night, dearest. I'm falling asleep now."

"Good night, Jeffrey. Sweet dreams."

14

"You were born you," Jeffrey had said. "You are a unique and charming person. . . ." All through the month of January I kept hearing those words. I would hear them during the day, as I mooned away in class, and I would hear them in my head at night before falling asleep. I was born me, but who *was* that? Not Marilyn Monroe and not Albert Einstein. Not Shirley, not Leonard, and not even a very clear reflection of grandparents and relatives. Who was Heidi, and what would she become? The mystery continued.

But there was one thing that was changing me—by power of example—and that was Jeffrey's determination. I would stand in front of theaters, watching him dance, and realize how much stamina it took to do that. I would comb secondhand book stores with him, looking for books on the theater. I would stand backstage while Jeffrey auditioned. Thanks, fella, that will be all. . . . That's all for now. . . . Do we have your phone number? . . . All for today, dear, thanks so much. God! If it had been me, I would have given up. But not Jeffrey. He hung in there—and the fact that he did was doing something strange to me.

I mean, what had I, Heidi, ever worked at? Nothing. And what had I ever aspired to? Nothing, nothing, nothing. Shirley had been like an eraser in my life, wiping me off the blackboard—but now all that was going to change. What was it that I loved better than anything else in the world, I asked myself. DOGS. And to handle dogs, one did not need to be either beautiful or brilliant. To handle dogs, as a matter of fact, one needed only to like dogs. Dogs . . . I kept saying to myself. Is there a future in that?

Maybe. In the sense that even though I was not smart enough to be a vet, I could always be a vet's assistant. Or a trainer. Or a handler. If worse came to worse, I could simply be a professional dog walker—someone who charged into the park each morning with a bevy of dogs on leashes. One girl in my neighborhood could walk eight dogs at a time. Not a bad way to make a living, and a lot of fresh air too.

January snowed and rained and sleeted its way into February—and Jeffrey kept on dancing. But his Friday nights at my house were doing him good. He would sleep for hours and hours, till ten in the morning sometimes, and I would always be on hand when he woke—with a tray of coffee and croissants. We were developing an intimacy that was so wonderful—and yet it was not intimate at all. Where I wanted to be was in that guest room with him, in that bed with him, but I never could have said so. Jeffrey loved me as a sister, as he had once explained. Jeffrey loved me as a friend.

Then, during the first week of March, something awful happened.

It began innocently enough—with me and Jeffrey going down to the Village to see *Now, Voyager*, an old Bette Davis film. It was one of Jeffrey's favorites and was playing at a small theater near Greenwich Avenue. I loved this movie, loved everything about it—and when it was over Jeffrey and I began to walk towards a coffeehouse near the Hudson River. It was a place he knew about called The Bountiful Bean, and it had live entertainment. Well, we never got to the coffeehouse. Because all of a sudden we were being followed—by two young hoods—and the faster we walked, the faster they walked too. The trouble was, the street we were on was almost deserted. And the night was very dark. We were on the point of running, when the hoods caught up with us. "Hey, faggot," one of them said.

A chill went down my spine as I realized that something terrible was about to happen. I had thought that they wanted to mug us, rob us, but not at all. What they wanted was Jeffrey.

"Hey, faggot," said the first guy, "can you spare a few bucks?"

Jeffrey turned to face them. They were both white kids, in their teens, and they looked very tough. And dangerous. "Jeffrey . . ." I began.

"Beat it," Jeffrey said to the first kid. "I'm not giving you anything."

"Oh, I bet you have plenty to give," said the second guy. "Plenty."

"Get out of our way," Jeffrey said firmly. "My girlfriend and I will not be threatened."

"Girlfriend?" shrieked the first guy. *"Girlfriend?* Hey listen, Michael. The fag's got a *girlfriend."*

And with that, they jumped him.

Even now, remembering all this, I cannot understand why those two hoods attacked Jeffrey. Maybe they wanted to beat someone up, and he presented an opportunity. Or maybe they just hated gays. At any rate, they knocked him to the ground and began to hammer him with their fists. I screamed for help, and then, when I realized that there *was* no help— that we were quite alone—I joined in the fight. I mean, I tackled one of those guys and sank my teeth into his ankle. He screamed, and tossed me away as though I was a kitten. I landed up against a car. But I charged right back, because I was not merely angry, I was insane. I wanted to kill them.

"Get out of here, Heidi!" Jeffrey was yelling. "Run, run!"

But I couldn't run, because the person I loved most in the world was flat on his back on the sidewalk, being bashed and beaten. Over and over again, I charged at the hoods, and over and over they tossed me away. Then something fantastic happened. Jeffrey fought back.

I don't know when I realized that this was happening, but all of a sudden Jeffrey was fighting back like Muhammad Ali. He was all fists and rage—and not a little bit of technique—as he bashed one of the hoods' heads on the sidewalk and then started to beat up the other. Two against one—and yet Jeffrey was winning, Jeffrey was fighting, and not only fighting, but like a pro.

"Kill them!" I screamed. "Massacre them, Jeffrey!"

I don't know what happened next, but suddenly the two thugs had taken to their heels and were running down the street. One had lost his jacket and was running in shirt sleeves. The other had lost a shoe.

I looked at Jeffrey, who was sitting on the curb in a kind of daze. His head was streaming blood. "Let's get to a hospital," I said.

He shook his head vaguely. "I'm . . . all right. Just give me a minute."

"No, Jeffrey. You need a doctor."

I ran out into the middle of the street and there, miraculously, was a cab. At first, the driver didn't want to take us—but I made such a commotion that he had to. The nearest hospital, he said, was St. Vincent's.

I helped Jeffrey into the taxi. "The emergency room," I said to the driver. "And please make it fast."

Jeffrey had his head back against the car seat and his eyes were closed. I tried to stop his head wound from bleeding with a wad of Kleenex. "Don't stain that seat!" the driver said. "This is a new cab."

St. Vincent's was only a few blocks away, and I was so anxious to get Jeffrey into the emergency room that I gave the driver a ten and didn't ask for change. With my arm around Jeffrey, I staggered into the hospital.

After what seemed like hours, we were admitted into one of the emergency booths. Jeffrey looked very pale and sick, but I had stopped his head from bleeding. Then the curtain was pushed aside and a young doctor in a white jacket came in. He was very attractive, but I didn't like the look of him at all. "So what have we here?" he asked.

"My friend was attacked on the street," I explained. "Two boys tried to beat him up."

The doctor gazed at Jeffrey—at his bleached hair and fur jacket, at the eye shadow on his lids. "It figures," he said.

"What?"

He gave me a funny little smile. "I said, it figures, young lady. If you ask for trouble, you get it."

Go drown yourself, I wanted to say. Go give yourself a lethal dose of morphine. But since this was the only doctor we had, I bit my tongue. "Look—my friend needs help. He has a head wound."

"*I'll* make the diagnosis, if you don't mind," said the doctor. "Now, would you mind stepping outside?"

"No," I said, "I won't. Because this person is my friend and he's just been mugged. So I'm staying here."

That seemed to shut him up, because he turned from me and began to examine Jeffrey—who by now was lying back on the examining table. He looked terrible.

"The wound will need a few stitches," the doctor said to me. "Other than that, he's all right."

I forced myself to watch as he cleaned and stitched the wound, and then I went outside and sat in the reception room for a while. All the strength I had had before was draining away. I felt faint.

"Would you like some coffee?" a young woman said to me. "There's a coffee machine in the hallway."

I nodded, and she brought me a container of coffee with milk in it. I didn't even know who she was, and never got a chance to find out. Just a good Samaritan, I guess.

Jeffrey rested in the little booth for an hour. Then a nurse brought him out to me. "Bloody but unbowed," he said with a weak smile. "Like Lawrence of Arabia."

I put my arms around him. "Oh, Jeffrey . . ."

"It's OK," he said, his head buried in my coat. "It's happened before."

"But this time you fought back. You did, Jeffrey! You fought back."

He stared at me. "It's true. I fought back."

"Two against one!"

"Right," he said, "right."

"I'm proud of you," I said.

With our arms around each other, we walked out to the street. It was cold and rainy and miserable, but something inside me was singing.

"You fought back, Jeffrey," I kept saying to him. "You fought back."

15

Jeffrey recovered. His head wound healed, and the bruises on his face disappeared, and within a few weeks he seemed to have forgotten the incident. But I hadn't—because I had seen now, firsthand, what Jeffrey was up against in the world. However, the way he fought back had revealed something to me, and it seemed very profound. Jeffrey was not really effeminate. Inside, he was as male as the two kids who had tried to beat him up. Effeminacy was something he put on, like a garment or a disguise. Why he chose to act that way, I did not know—but it wasn't the real him.

"Where did you learn to fight like that?" I asked two nights later. We were sitting in Danny's Coffee Shop, and Jeffrey still looked very pale. One of his eyes was blackened, and there was a bruise on his right cheekbone.

"Sister Margaret taught me. When I was eight."

I started to laugh. "Oh, Jeffrey . . ."

"It's true. She saw that I was going to have a hard time with the other kids, because they thought I was a sissy, and so she taught me to box."

"Who *is* this nun? She sounds unreal."

"Heidi, Sister is an amazing character. She's very big, almost six feet, but graceful. First she taught me to box, and then she taught me to tap dance. We practiced in the basement most of the time, but the tiles in the boys' bathroom were so terrific for dancing—I mean, they made such a lovely, clicking sound—that sometimes we'd practice there too. The thing is, she knew her stuff. Her father had been in vaudeville."

I took a sip of my coffee. "No kidding?"

"The whole family had been in show business at one time or another. So Sister could dance and sing as well as the best of them. She taught me all the routines she knew, and the rest I learned from the movies. God, I loved her! Every night, for four years, she came into my cubicle to kiss me good night. Like a mother."

"A nun with a vaudeville background. That's terrific."

"Oh, I don't mean that her family were headliners. They never got to be famous or anything. But there was a long tradition of show business in the family, and she was the first to break it. By going into a convent, I mean."

I sat there, trying to picture a six-foot-tall nun doing a tap dance—and failed. "Was it she who wanted you to be a priest?"

Jeffrey looked startled. "Oh no, not at all. That was something I dreamed up myself, when I was twelve. It seemed like a . . . solution."

"To being gay?"

"Yes, sweetie. Exactly."

"But you're not sorry now, are you Jeffrey?"

He smiled. "I'm glad to be me."

As we continued to drink our coffee, I realized that in some ways Jeffrey had had a better childhood than I—in the sense that Sister Margaret only wanted him to be himself. She had not tried to make him into a doctor, or a lawyer—or a priest—she had simply taught him to defend himself and to tap dance. And wasn't that what parenting was all about? To help the kid become himself? If only Leonard and Shirley had ever looked at me, at Heidi, I might not have turned out to be such a wreck.

Since Jeffrey's fur jacket had been torn during the fight, we went together to Grandma's Attic to buy him a new one—and what we chose was an old Persian lamb jacket with full sleeves. I know this sounds sissy, but it wasn't. It looked wonderful on him. For myself, I bought another vest and a suede cowboy jacket with fringe. At the last minute, I also bought a belt that had been made in Arizona—one with fake silver medallions. It looked good with my jeans.

"What is this?" Shirley said, when she saw the new purchases. "You're going into a rodeo?"

As usual, I felt anger flaring inside of me. "This was once a very good jacket. An expensive jacket."

"For a cowboy, yes. Not for a young lady who goes to Spencer."

"Mom," I said, my voice shaking a little. "I have got to be allowed to dress like *me*."

"And what is you?" she demanded. "A cowboy? An Indian? Heidi, your father works like a dog to give you the very best in life, and all you do is hang around thrift shops. It makes me want to cry."

So cry, I felt like saying. Cry your eyes out, because I am *not* going to turn into a miniature Bobo Lewis. That's what you'd like—someone with piles of strawberry-blond hair and masses of makeup, someone who stuffs her fat legs into pantyhose and whose boobs are always falling out of some dress— but I will NOT be that kind of person. I will jump off a building first. Aloud, I said, "I can't talk about this anymore."

"Well, neither can I!" said Shirley. "I've talked about it until I'm a wreck. How do you think I feel every time you go down in the elevator? Every time someone in the building sees you?"

"God!" I screamed. "What does it matter who

sees me! I'm not Princess Diana!"

"Don't be fresh with me, Heidi!"

"Leave me alone. Please, please leave me alone."

"You will not wear that cowboy jacket in the elevator," said Shirley. "If you want to wear that jacket, you will walk down the back stairs."

"Go to hell," I said. And then she slapped me.

It was only the second time in our lives that this had happened—and so we were both stunned. I went to my room, she went to hers, but I think the shock was equally bad for both of us. Shirley was not a physically violent person, and yet she had hit me. And I was a person not used to being hit.

All that day, and far into the night, I thought about leaving home. Jeffrey had told me about the homeless kids in Chicago—kids who are on the move all the time lest truant officers pick them up, kids who sleep in abandoned buildings and beg for money on the street—and while I couldn't see myself living that way, I would do it if he would come with me. Shirley and I would be at each other's throats pretty soon, and I didn't want that to happen.

As I said, it was March now, and while I had bought Jeffrey a sleeping bag, a good one, he was cold all the time. He'd stop dancing in the street, because of the cold, and take shelter in a restaurant or bar. He would spend hours on Friday nights in Shirley's bathtub. Jeffrey just couldn't get warm anymore, and was talking about taking a bus to Florida.

124

He had a friend there named Kevin.

I would have to make his life better, I told myself, but how? Sneak him into the apartment every night after Shirley had gone to sleep? Let him sleep in Leonard's apartment while Leonard was at the office? No, too dangerous, too risky. And then it hit me: I would find him a job.

Not just any job, but a job in a Broadway show. And how, you may ask, did I intend to do that? By getting the advice of the one and only person I knew in show business—Janet Margolis.

Miss Margolis was our Music and Drama teacher, and, like all the teachers at Spencer, she was underpaid and overworked. Spencer, as a matter of fact, paid such awful salaries that we had a very odd faculty. Mr. Potts, the Ancient History teacher, looked around fourteen years old because he was simply a graduate student from Columbia—and Frau Schneider, who had been born in Frankfurt, taught us German on the days when she remembered to show up. Mr. Wannings, the Religion teacher, was really an unfrocked minister from the Episcopal church. And then there was Janet Margolis. Pretty and vivacious, with wonderful clothes, Miss Margolis had been in two Broadway musicals and was biding her time at Spencer until another job turned up. She taught us music and drama, and her classes were great. I mean, they were not the kind of classes in which you had to memorize speeches from Shakespeare. In Miss Margolis's classes we did numbers from *Cats* and scenes from Woody Allen movies.

I approached her one Tuesday morning in the school library, where she was reading a book by John Updike. As always, she looked terrific—her red hair piled on top of her head, her clothes patterned and layered. "Posthippie" is what Veronica Bangs used to call it, and she was right. "Miss Margolis . . ." I began.

She looked up from her book and smiled at me. "Well hello, Heidi. How are you?"

"Great," I said, sitting down at the table beside her. "Do you have a minute?"

She took off her horn-rimmed glasses and gave me another smile. "Of course. What can I do for you?"

Liberate my friend from sleeping in an abandoned building, I wanted to say. But instead, I said, "I need some advice."

"Shoot."

I hesitated for a minute. "Well . . . it's this way. I have a very dear friend who is trying to break into show business, and he's having a hard time. I mean, he's dancing on the street and everything, trying to be discovered. He's homeless."

Because Miss Margolis was a superior type of woman, she did not say, Why Heidi, how could you have met such a person? Or, Does your mother know about this? Or, You shouldn't mingle with such types. Instead, she said, "Interesting. What kind of dancing does he do?"

"Tap, mostly. Gene Kelly style. And he sings too—beautifully."

"And you want me to send him to my agent."

"Well, yes. Sure! That would be great!"

Miss Margolis bit her lower lip for a second. "How much do you know about show business?" she asked.

"Not much."

"That's what I thought. But you *do* know that it's tough to get a job?"

"Yes, I know that."

"Ninety percent of Actors Equity is permanently unemployed."

"My friend is brilliant, Miss Margolis, really. He's great."

"Has he tried off-Broadway?"

"No. It's the big time he wants."

She thought for a moment. "OK. Why don't you take me to wherever he's dancing, and I'll have a look at him. It doesn't mean I can get him a job, but maybe I could do something."

"Miss Margolis, you're a terrific person. Everyone in this school thinks so."

She laughed. "Let's have dinner together tomorrow night. And then I'll watch your friend strut his stuff."

16

Miss Margolis and I had dinner at a place called Jumbo's, on 46th Street, and while we ate she told me all about herself. She was from Seattle, and had come East a few years ago with a degree in dance and drama and no money at all. At once, she had landed a chorus job in a show called *Serendipity*, and after that other jobs had followed. She was a totally self-made woman, which I admired, and I also loved the way she was dressed. A long wool skirt with black boots. A cashmere turtleneck sweater with another, looser, sweater over it. Beads, earrings, and that terrific hair piled high upon her head. She was definitely posthippie.

"You've had a wonderful life," I said, as our desserts arrived.

"I don't know, Heidi. It's been rough at times."

"But you've done what you wanted to. You've been yourself."

Miss Margolis thought about this for a minute. "Yes, I've always been myself. Life is too short to do otherwise."

Jeffrey was dancing tonight in front of the Shubert Theatre, and I had not told him we were coming. In fact, I'd said that I was getting a cold and might not be coming downtown at all. I wanted Miss Margolis to observe him without his knowing it.

We walked over to the Shubert Theatre in a chilling wind. It was whipping around street corners and pulling people's hats off. It was fierce. Customers were already going into the Shubert for the evening show, and the sidewalk was crowded. In the center of the crowd was Jeffrey, dancing to "Get Happy" on the tape recorder.

"Forget your troubles, c'mon get happy," sang Judy, as Jeffrey did his slow, lazy, casual tap dance. He looked wonderful, so handsome, and I felt my heart beat faster as I watched him work. Miss Margolis and I stood at the edge of the crowd, where he could not see us. I saw that she was watching him intently.

The wind was whipping newspapers down the street, and a man's hat rolled by, but Jeffrey just kept on dancing. It was funny, but the Persian lamb jacket didn't look sissy on him. It just looked stylish. His cheeks were red from the cold, but his feet kept

129

tapping away. People threw coins into his hat, and kept going into the theater.

After about fifteen minutes, Miss Margolis said, "There's a place across the street. Let's go there."

So we went into a small dark café that had a piano player, and sat down at the bar. Miss Margolis ordered a brandy and I ordered a Coke. She lit a cigarette and puffed on it for a minute.

I didn't want to rush her, because I could see that she was thinking, evaluating, deciding what she was going to say to me. I hadn't known whether she'd liked him or not, because her face was impassive as she watched him, but I couldn't see how she wouldn't like Jeffrey. He had such style.

Miss Margolis took a sip of her brandy. "Heidi . . ."

I was sitting very close to her on my bar stool, so close that I could smell the perfume she was wearing. So close that I could see deeply into her eyes. "Yes?"

"Heidi, look. I don't want to disappoint you, because I can tell you care about that boy, but honey . . . he's not all that great."

"He's not?" I said, wondering if I had heard her correctly.

"No dear, he's not. I mean, boys like that are a dime a dozen. You see them at every open call. And it's not that they can't dance, because all of them can. It's just that they're lacking that 'something extra' you always hear about."

"I don't understand."

"Your friend can dance, but so can a million other kids. The auditions are crowded with them, the producers' offices are crowded with them. There's just too many of them, Heidi."

"I see," I said slowly.

"I know this is hurting you, and I don't like to do that—but there's nothing unusual about this boy. He's just another tap dancer. And by the way, he'd do better not to bleach his hair. It looks awful."

I felt like she had punched me in the stomach. "So you think he doesn't have a chance?"

"I didn't say that. For all I know, he may get into a show someday. But he's lacking that extra quality—the thing you see in a Mark Morris or a Tommy Tune. Do you understand what I mean?"

"No. I don't."

"I'm hurting you," she said.

"No," I said after a few seconds, "you're being honest with me, and I appreciate that. But all this is a shock. Because for months now, I've thought he was great."

"He's good. But he doesn't stand out."

Miss Margolis took me uptown in a cab, and for most of the way we didn't talk. The things she had said had devastated me—but I was still glad she had said them. Because if it was true that Jeffrey wasn't that good, then he and I would have to rethink everything.

When the cab pulled up in front of my building, Miss Margolis took my hand. "I'll go on to Ninety-sixth Street, where I live. And Heidi? I'm sorry if I hurt you. You're in love with that boy, aren't you?"

"Yes. I am."

A sad smile crossed her face. "Good luck, then. And good night."

I lay awake that night, thinking of all the things she had told me—and wondering who Tommy Tune and Mark Morris were. Did Miss Margolis have that quality she called "something extra"? Probably. But Jeffrey did not.

It's only one opinion, I said to myself. One opinion out of thousands. Suppose she's wrong, and he's really a genius? No. If he was a genius she would have seen it right away. . . . But if he isn't that good, what will become of him? He can't dance on the street forever. He can't go on sleeping in abandoned buildings. He needs a home and someone to love him. He needs *me*.

By morning I had gotten exactly two hours sleep and was in a rage. Because what Miss Margolis had not taken into account was that Jeffrey was only twenty years old. Wasn't there time for him to grow, to improve, to refine his style? I sat through breakfast with Shirley in silence, as my mind went round and round these things. Half of me was infuriated with Miss Margolis—but the other half was afraid she was right.

School started at eight-thirty, so at eight o'clock I began to throw stuff into my book bag. "Don't wear that awful coat!" Shirley called to me from her bedroom. "Right!" I called back. "Absolutely!"

Wearing That Coat and my green tam-o'-shanter, I went down in the elevator and made my way to school. It was a typical March day, with wind racing down the avenues and a sky that was swept with dark clouds. A million school kids, it seemed, were hurrying to school. A million men with briefcases were boarding buses.

I was early for my first class, English III, so I wandered down to the gym, which is in the basement. And there, for some reason, was Miss Margolis— watching basketball practice. Why she was watching such a thing, I do not know—but when our eyes met, there was a new kind of understanding between us. Hold on, her gaze said to me. Hold on, Heidi. Because in the long run, everything works out.

17

Dogs, I said to myself, it has got to be dogs. Why else have I spent my life picking up strays and taking them to shelters? Why else do I still keep in my closet books with titles like *You and Your Schnauzer*. For all I know, I may have to support Jeffrey someday—and dogs are the way to do it. A trainer, a handler, a vet's assistant. A groomer in a dog grooming parlor.

I could always get work in a shelter, of course, but most of those people didn't get paid—and it was money I was thinking of now, because something told me I would not be going to college. And what would happen to my father if I did not go? A heart attack? A fatal stroke? No, I told myself, he will bear up. We all will.

Shirley's trips to Scarsdale had come to an end.

She had had enough of bridge, and couldn't get a good night's sleep at Bobo's house. The sounds of the country kept her awake. So Jeffrey's hot bubble baths were over, and his long nights of sleeping in the guest room. Gone were his morning trays of coffee and croissants. Gone, our midnight talks. The weather was milder now, but Jeffrey was still cold. It was the last time in his life, he said, that he would ever live like a vagrant. Terrible things had happened in his building during the past months. The alcoholic lawyer had died, the woman with the cat had mysteriously disappeared. And a whole new group of people had moved in on the floor below. Jeffrey was sure that these types were going to set the house on fire because they burned trash in wire baskets to keep warm.

It was almost spring, and I am one of those people who fall apart in the springtime. The mild weather affects me and makes me absentminded. I begin to listen to music again and take walks in Central Park. In the spring New York is a magical place, with flower vendors on corners and the streets washed with soft rain. Suddenly the store windows look fresh and interesting. Suddenly the sun bounces off buildings. In two short months I would be liberated from that prison called school, and would be free to spend all my time with Jeffrey. My latest idea was to enroll him in a dance school, so he could improve his technique.

You may be thinking that by now I had calmed down about Jeffrey—but not at all. I still felt as emotional about him as I had in the beginning, and there were nights when I lay awake with my heart hurting, and my head hurting, and every part of me hurting because I couldn't have him. Jeffrey, I thought, you are everything I want—gentleness, kindness, humor, talent—and more than anything, we have fun together. I know that you care for me, because whenever we meet your face lights up like a child's. And only last week you bought me a bunch of yellow tulips, to usher in the spring. Yet when I asked you once—casually—if gay people ever turn straight, you burst out laughing and asked me if straight people ever turn gay. So that, as they say, was that.

I was cutting gym these days—having forged a note in Shirley's handwriting saying that Heidi was undergoing dentistry—so that Jeffrey and I could meet in the early afternoons. We would meet in front of the Plaza Hotel and stroll into Central Park, munching on hamburgers, drinking orange drink. Dogs, babies, kids playing ball—and the carousel, where Jeffrey and I would ride round and round with the children, trying to catch the brass ring.

One sunny afternoon we were sitting on a bench in the park, reading the trade papers, when a little dog ran past us. In a minute he was back, looking confused, and then he was off again. Being me, I knew instantly that 1) the dog had no owner 2) he was desperate 3) he needed me. So I ran over to some children who were petting him, and picked him up. To my surprise, he didn't protest, but started to lick my face. "What are you?" I said. "A Norfolk terrier? A Cairn?"

I walked back to Jeffrey, holding the dog in my arms. He was very small and the color of taffy. He was also thin.

"Oh my God!" said Jeffrey. "What have you got there?"

"No collar and no leash," I declared, sitting down on the bench. "Another stray. New York is full of them."

"Oh no," Jeffrey groaned.

"Never mind. Give him your hamburger."

Having just been about to bite into a hamburger he had bought from a vendor, Jeffrey looked dubious. But, with a shrug, he gave the dog the hamburger—bun and ketchup and all.

"I'll call him Happy," I said.

Jeffrey and I gazed at Happy, who was devouring the hamburger like there was no tomorrow. He was neither Cairn nor Norfolk terrier—but an interesting combination of both. The minute he had eaten, he was back on my lap. "I *love* this dog," I said to Jeffrey. "I'm going to keep him."

"But Heidi . . ."

"I know, I know, it will drive Shirley wild. But he's an omen."

"Of what, for heaven's sake?"

"I don't know. Of the future, maybe. I keep feeling that whatever I'm going to do with my life will involve dogs. And here we suddenly have a dog. Out of the blue."

"He probably belongs to someone."

"Are you kidding? No collar and no leash. And he's skinny. Nope. He's been abandoned."

Jeffrey started to laugh. "All you need, my darling, is another stray. First me, and then Happy."

"It's OK," I said, not looking at him. "I can love you both."

"A suggestion. Take him to the vet before you take him home to your mother—for shots and everything."

So we hailed a cab and took Happy down to the Animal Medical Center, by the East River. All during the drive, he sat on my lap gazing out of the window. He had such a good temperament! And as we sat in the large reception room, waiting to see a vet, Happy didn't even bark at the other dogs. There was something about him that was cool and resourceful and tough.

To make a long story short, it cost me exactly eighty-five dollars for an examination and shots. They bathed Happy for us too—and I paid with Shirley's MasterCard, which she had loaned me just the other day. The trouble was, she had loaned it to me so that I could buy a raincoat.

The Medical Center had given us a collar and a leash, and by late afternoon Jeffrey and I were standing on a corner in the East 60's. He was on his way to an audition downtown—and I, with some trepidation, was on my way home with a dog.

"I hope it goes well," Jeffrey said to me. "I hope she lets you keep him."

"Jeffrey—I'm keeping him if I have to take a separate apartment."

"I'm glad we found him together."

I didn't know what he meant by that. I just reached up and kissed him, very quickly. "I'll meet you tomorrow afternoon, in front of the Plaza. Happy will be with me."

"Good-bye for now, dearest."

"Good-bye."

Happy and I took another cab home, and once again he sat on my lap, watching the sights go by. He was terribly intelligent and alert. The vet had said he was around two years old.

"Got a dog there, I see," said the new elevator man, Albert, as we ascended to the fifteenth floor.

"Correct," I replied. "His name is Happy."

"Which is what your mother *won't* be when she sees him, right?"

I gave Albert a dirty look and got off at my floor. Happy was pulling on the leash, sniffing this, sniffing that. He seemed very excited.

Unfortunately, I had forgotten my keys, so I had

to ring the doorbell. Shirley answered it, wearing a mumu she had bought in Hawaii years ago. Her hair was in rollers and she had on her reading glasses.

"Where have you . . ." she began. And then she saw the dog.

I let go of Happy's leash and he began to run all around the living room, sniffing, investigating. Without looking at Shirley, I took off my cowboy jacket and my green tam. I went into the kitchen for a glass of water.

Shirley followed me. "What is that out there?" she asked.

"What does it look like? It's a dog."

"A dog?" said Shirley, as though the word was a foreign one. "A *dog*? What in the name of God are you doing with a dog?"

"I found him in the park and I'm keeping him. His name is Happy." I poured myself a second glass of water.

"Now look here . . ." Shirley began. Her voice was shaking.

"He's been to the vet, and tomorrow I'm going to buy him a little coat at Bloomingdale's—so he can go down in the elevator without embarrassing you. He's part Cairn."

"Heidi, you know that I'm . . ."

"That's never been proved," I said. "You've

never even been to an allergist. Bobo has a dog, and you never sneeze when you're at her house. So now we have a dog, too."

Happy raced into the kitchen and jumped up on Shirley, wagging his tail. She pushed him away. "I'm calling your father."

"So call. Call the president, if you want to. In Washington."

"Don't you be fresh with me."

"Call the FBI, the CIA."

"Stop this rudeness!"

"I need a dog," I said to her. "Someone to love me."

Shirley's mouth dropped open. Then tears—quick, unexpected—came down her cheeks. They were not the crocodile tears she usually shed. They were real.

"No one has ever loved a child as much as I love you," she said quietly. "And if you don't know it, you're a fool."

She went into her bedroom and closed the door—and I was left standing there in a state of shock. Because it was true. She did love me. She didn't understand me, she didn't *see* me, but she loved me. And so did my father. I mean—God!—who had ever seen *them*? Rosalie, my grandmother, had ridden over my mother's life like a truck. And Leonard's family, who were immigrants, had put him to work when he was fifteen. My father hadn't even finished high school—and my mother's dreams of being a decorator had been ended by marriage. Who had seen them?

All of a sudden, I felt compassion for my parents—and this was such a new feeling that I sank down on the kitchen stool, amazed. And as though real people were passing before my eyes, I saw a long line of relatives marching through the kitchen—grandparents, cousins, uncles, aunts—with no one ever understanding anyone else. Rosalie had probably found Shirley's values just as weird as Shirley found mine. And my Russian grandfather had probably suffered over the fact that Leonard hadn't gone to night school. They wanted him to finish school at night, and even go on to college, but he refused.

I went into Shirley's room. She was sitting on the side of the bed, staring into space. Her face was stained with tears. "Mom . . ."

"You can keep the dog. I never said you couldn't."

"Mom, listen . . ."

"Just be sure he's had shots."

"I already took him. This afternoon."

"He'll need to be walked three times a day."

"I can do that," I said. "Don't worry."

But what I wanted to say was that I knew she loved me—and that in some way I could never express, I loved her. I wanted to make peace with her, and hold her close to me. I wanted to tell her about those people who had marched through the kitchen.

All I said, however, was, "Thanks, Mom. I appreciate it."

18

During the first week of May, something strange happened. Jeffrey began to mention two people called Peter and Eugene. At first, their names popped in and out of his conversation so quickly that I barely noticed them. But then, slowly, the words became more apparent. Jeffrey was going down to the Village to have dinner with Peter and Eugene. Jeffrey was going to spend the night there. I pricked up my ears and began to listen. Peter and Eugene were dancers whom Jeffrey had met at an audition. They had a small place in the East Village, only two rooms, but they would let Jeffrey sleep on the couch. They were both twenty-three years old.

I tried to be cool about Peter and Eugene for exactly one week—nodded and smiled whenever Jeffrey mentioned their names, said things like, "Yes, that sounds interesting," or "Have a nice time with your friends," but something inside me was wavering. Peter and Eugene had met at ballet school, Jeffrey explained. Unlike him, they had formal training. Eugene had never been in a show, but Peter had understudied one of the dancers in *A Chorus Line*. "Are Peter and Eugene gay?" I had finally asked—and Jeffrey burst out laughing. "But of course! What did you think?"

So once again I realized that there was a special club on this earth called "being gay" and that I was not a member. And this knowledge hurt me so much that I came right out and asked Jeffrey if I could meet his new friends. He had looked surprised—but the next night he had taken me down to their apartment on East 10th Street. It was a nice apartment, filled with interesting things, and there was a poster of Baryshnikov over the fireplace. I walked in there with Jeffrey and Happy, prepared to hate Peter and Eugene as much as I had ever hated anyone—but I couldn't. They both kissed me on the cheek and said how delighted they were to meet me. They petted Happy and gave him a ball to play with. They served us white wine and little canapés.

What did I expect? That they would be dressed like women? That they would be wearing makeup? *Wrong.* Because while Eugene was slightly effeminate, Peter was not. Peter, in fact, was one hundred percent masculine, and terribly good-looking. They

145

were both articulate and read a lot of books. They had good music on the stereo.

I could not hate them—but at the same time, something told me that they were replacing me, that they were providing Jeffrey with the one thing I could not give him: a home. He slept there all the time now, and helped with the shopping and household chores. The three of them went to auditions together, and ate dinner at a place called The Flamenco every Friday night. Peter and Eugene had introduced Jeffrey to their friends. Eugene had bought him a new pair of tap shoes.

Feeling obsolete, I walked Happy along the East River promenade, and one day took him to a grooming parlor to have him clipped. The owner of the parlor, Mrs. Geary, said that he was more Norfolk than Cairn. So I bought a book on Norfolk terriers and began to study Happy's ancestry. Terriers had once been called Earth Dogs, and most of them had been used for digging tunnels and going after prey, like rats. The Norfolk was a variant of the Norwich. "They are brave, scrappy little dogs," the book said. "They are loyal and have a fire inside that cannot be quenched."

Maxie the poodle had been Leonard's dog, not mine. But Happy was one hundred percent mine, and it made a difference. I thought back over my life and realized that until Happy I had never had anything to call my own. I had never kept a diary be-

146

cause I knew that Shirley would read it. Had never kept photos of friends because photos would have produced an inquisition. . . . I had never dressed the way I wanted to dress or said the words I wanted to say. But now everything was changing. The point was: This revolution did not have to be a violent one. I could become whoever I was going to be in a peaceful way. Mahatma Gandhi Rosenbloom.

I went back to Grandma's Attic and bought a repertoire of spring clothes. Boys' chinos and two cotton vests. A fantastic pair of brown riding boots. And, lest the whole thing become too masculine, a long silk skirt with flowers on it.

Jeffrey rarely phoned me at the apartment—but one afternoon the phone rang and it was him. Shirley was at the Red Cross, doing her volunteer work. "Jeffrey?" I said. "Is anything wrong? You sound so funny."

"No, no, no," he said breathlessly. "It's just that I need to see you. Something has happened."

"Something good?" I inquired cautiously. His voice was so odd. I hardly recognized it.

"Oh yes, something good! Something wonderful, in fact. Can you meet me at the coffee shop?"

"I'll be there in thirty minutes."

I threw on my cowboy jacket and put a leash on my dog. I went down to the street, hailed a cab, and settled back against the leather seat with Happy on my lap. He's found a job, I said to myself, Jeffrey has found a job. He's gotten a part in a musical or a play. An agent has discovered him, or maybe a producer. Jeffrey is going to be on Broadway.

He was already at Danny's Coffee Shop when I arrived, sitting at our special table near the window. I raced inside, pulling Happy behind me on the leash. Jeffrey grabbed me in a bear hug. "Good news!"

I sat down at the table and tucked Happy underneath, hoping that no one would notice him. "Tell me," I said. "I can't wait."

"I'm *trying* to."

"No, don't tell me, let me guess. You've gotten a part in a show. You've found a job."

Jeffrey looked astonished. "Is that what you thought? Oh no, that's not it! It's something even better. I'm going to California."

"Where?" I said slowly.

"Los Angeles, darling. Lotus Land. Peter and Eugene are driving out in ten days because Peter's gotten a job in a TV special. They're borrowing a car from Peter's father, in Connecticut. We've even got a place to stay out there, right in the heart of Hollywood! This is such an *opportunity* for me, Heidi. To meet agents and choreographers, to get the lay of the land. And I'd so much rather work out there than here. It's cold here."

"No, it's not," I said. "It's May."

"Cold in the winter, I mean. And I hate the cold,

absolutely hate it. I always have."

"But you grew up in Illinois."

"Exactly!" said Jeffrey, summoning the waiter. "Let's celebrate, love. Let's order something special."

It is strange to feel that you are dying as you sit in a coffee shop, chatting with someone. Strange to feel that your life has come to an end while you watch a friend eat his sandwich. All of a sudden a curtain had been drawn over that thing I called the future.

"How long will you be gone?" I asked.

"Don't know, love, a few months maybe. We've taken a place near Sunset Boulevard. . . . Who knows—you may be seeing me on television within the year. Keep your eye on the tube, darling! Keep your eye on the tube!"

He was being effeminate—the way he always was when he felt unsure of himself, or had to face a new situation. He was being effeminate and silly—and I hated it.

"Maybe you'll never come back," I said, trying to keep my voice casual. "Maybe you'll like it out there."

"Wall-to-wall swimming pools. A suntan all year long." Cheerfully, Jeffrey ordered us more coffee.

The thing that stunned me was not that he was going away—or even that he was going to California. I mean, I could have flown out to California to see him, and stayed with Veronica. The thing that devastated me was that he seemed to have no feelings for me. It was as though all the months and all the hardships had never happened. As though we had never been close, never shared our lives or our dreams. He was leaving me behind as if I was an old shoe.

". . . choreographers," Jeffrey was saying. "Some of the best in the world. And they say that Streisand may be doing a series of specials, too."

I rose to my feet. "I've got to be going now."

"Must you, love? Well, all right. Let's have lunch tomorrow, OK?"

I couldn't believe his behavior. And as I watched him during the next week—shopping for clothes, having his hair bleached even lighter at a men's hair salon, making plans with Peter and Eugene—I felt like I didn't know him anymore. He was silly and superficial. He talked about what a great tan he would get in L.A. and what super parties he would give. God! He even bought me a map of Hollywood and showed me where his new house was. Right near Sunset Boulevard.

A hundred times I wanted to take his hand and ask him what was going on, ask him why he had changed. But I didn't. And then I began to wonder if I had ever known him at all. Maybe Jeffrey was someone I had invented for myself—some sad little knight in shining armor.

19

A few days later Happy and I stood on the sidewalk outside of Peter and Eugene's place on 10th Street. Peter, Eugene and Jeffrey were packing the last of their things into the Chevrolet. They were in high spirits and kept giggling and joking with each other. I, meanwhile, stood on the sidelines with a smile on my face that could have been pasted on with glue.

"We're off to see the Wizard!" Jeffrey was singing. And every so often, the other two joined in. No one looked at me, particularly. No one wondered what I was feeling. Happy sat on the sidewalk and watched the activities. In the past weeks he and I had grown very close.

"That's it," Peter said to Jeffrey. "If we put anything more in that car it will sink."

"Time to go," said Eugene, smiling at me.

151

Peter and Eugene came over and shook hands with me. Then all three of them stood in a row in front of me, as though I was inspecting the troops. "So good-bye and good luck," I said to them. "And don't forget to write."

It was said ironically, of course, because I knew that none of them would write me. They would forget about me the minute the car was on its way. Something also told me that Jeffrey was not coming back to New York—because he had a new dream now called television. Yep, Jeffrey had decided that *this* was going to be his medium because, after all, it is just too hard to get into a Broadway show. Once it had been Broadway, now it was television. And after that, Jeffrey, I said silently, what happens after that? Will there always be a Heidi Rosenbloom around, to help you when you're desperate, to buy you a meal and cheer you up? Am I really that replaceable? Am I worth anything at all?

Peter and Eugene were in the car now, in the front seat, waiting for Jeffrey to say good-bye to me. He came over and put his hands on my shoulders. I noticed that he was wearing new jeans and a new shirt.

"Time to go," he said gaily. "Off to see the Wizard."

"Right," I said.

He was gazing at my haircut, which I had just had

152

trimmed at the barber's. "I'm *mad* about the way your hair looks today."

"Ah, come on, Jeffrey. You say that to all the boys."

It was supposed to be a joke, but neither of us laughed. "I'll send you postcards along the way," he said. "You know that, don't you?"

"Absolutely."

"And maybe when we get there, I'll give you a ring."

"Sure. I'll wait by the phone."

"Off to Sunset Boulevard! Me and Gloria Swanson, in drag."

"You and Bette Davis!"

"Me and Joan Crawford!"

"Say good-bye to Happy," I said.

Jeffrey knelt on the sidewalk and put his arms around the dog. And then, all of a sudden, he began to cry.

I knelt on the sidewalk with him and put my cheek against his. "Don't cry, please don't. I can't take it."

"I don't want to go. I don't want to leave you."

"It'll be all right, Jeffrey, I promise you."

"It's just such a good chance for me. Out there."

"I know."

"Oh God," he said. "Why am I doing this?"

Because you're a dreamer, I wanted to say. Because you're waiting to catch the brass ring as the carousel goes round. Because you're waiting to win the lottery and hit the jackpot. And how can anyone tell you that it will never happen, Jeffrey? How can anyone be that cruel?

Jeffrey kissed Happy on the top of his head. "Good-bye, little dog. Take care of Heidi."

"He will," I said.

He rose to his feet and wiped his tears away. But he was still crying.

I reached up and kissed him quickly. "Knock 'em dead, Jeffrey."

"You too, dearest. And listen—will you remember how special you are? How beautiful?"

A lump came into my throat. "Of course."

"I love you, Heidi."

And then he was gone, the Chevy pulling away from the curb, and Happy barking excitedly, as though to say good-bye. Off to Lotus Land, with Peter driving, and Eugene in the front seat chatting away, and Jeffrey waving to me through the rear window. I waved until the car was out of sight—then I started to walk uptown, taking with me a small dog and a broken heart. And it didn't matter that I understood him now—understood that his behavior was simply a means of breaking away—none of it really mattered, because Jeffrey Collins was gone.

20

There is a gold cross around my neck as I write this—even though my mother saw it once and had a fit—and whenever I go back to the theater district, to buy tickets for a show, I see Jeffrey there. I'm not thinking of him, and then suddenly I am—because just down the street is the ghost of a boy who is dancing. Yep, a tall boy with bleached blond hair is doing a tap dance, and people are throwing coins into his hat. He is wearing a fur jacket and has eye shadow on his lids.

The boy looks at me and smiles, and I say, "Can I buy you a cup of coffee?" "Lovely," he replies. "I'll be with you in a minute."

He never wrote me, you know, not once. But he had a right to go his own way, just as I have a right to go mine. I mean, sometimes you fall in love with

155

the wrong person and don't even know it. Sometimes you give your future away, rather than keeping it for yourself.

Somewhere out there, dancing on the pavement, is a boy who wants to be a star. And who am I to say that it will never happen? Maybe Lady Luck has smiled on Jeffrey, and maybe one night I'll turn on the television and see him dancing in the light of broken rainbows, dancing up a storm.

Jeffrey, I say in the privacy of my mind, it's all right now. Because I am everything you said.